Amberlin
Book One: Divine Destiny
by
W. Bradford Swift

I0548796

AMBERLIN: DIVINE DESTINY

First edition. July 17, 2018.

Written by W. Bradford Swift.

CHAPTER ONE
Whirlpool

THERE ARE ONLY TWO ways to live your life. One as though nothing is a miracle. The other is as though everything is a miracle. Albert Einstein

GOLDEN ACRES 1952

Seven-year-old Amberlin sashayed into the oversized bathroom, a towel wrapped around her slender frame. She peered over the side of the Victorian-style tub where her grandmother had recently finished drawing a few inches of bath water. She stepped onto the three-legged stool her Papa Herb had made for her when she was five so she could climb into the tub on her own even though in the last two years she'd grown beyond really needing it. She dropped the towel to the floor, then holding onto the towel rack, she gingerly tested the water with her right foot, expecting the water to be too hot. For once Rose had gotten the temperature just right though she wished the water was a little deeper. She eased herself into the water with a sigh and watched her rubber ducky float away by the miniature tsunami created by her entrance.

"I'll be in there in a couple minutes to check on you. Be sure you wash those golden locks of yours and clean behind your ears," her grandmother called from the next room. Several minutes elapsed with no sign of Rose. Amberlin finished cleaning herself, including her hair and ears, then played with ducky for a while. Still no Rose. Finally, she pulled the plug and let the soapy water begin to drain. She stayed in the tub, knowing the sound of the water would draw her grandmother away from her work and into the bathroom to be sure her hair was clean.

1

Amberlin watched as the ducky drifted towards the spiraling whirlpool as the water continued to drain from the tub. As the clockwise current of water drew the floating toy into its influence, she smiled and waved her index finger in a counterclockwise motion, then giggled as the spout changed direction, and the toy duck followed suit. After a few moments, Amberlin stopped her finger, and the water quickly resumed its customary clockwise motion, until once again she impressed her will upon the water. She continued playing like this for several moments, enchanted by the game without noticing Rose quietly observing her, until suddenly...

"What in God's name are you doing? Oh my Lord," Rose shrieked.

"Herb, Herb. Come in here at once," she yelled to her husband, but even before he arrived, she took matters into her own age-spotted hands, as she was accustomed to doing.

"You stop that right now, you hear. That's a bad girl." Rose grabbed Amberlin's hand with the offending index finger and slapped it sharply across the knuckles. "You mustn't do such things. Dear God... Herb, Herb. Are you coming?" Amberlin tried to stifle her cry of alarm and pain, but a whimper escaped despite her best effort. As she tried to pull her hand from danger, a pair of tears escaped coursing down her ruddy cheeks.

"What's all the ruckus about, Rose?" Herb Gentry asked as he hurried down the corridor from their bedroom.

"It's your granddaughter. It's started... already. She's only seven, and it's already begun. Do you have any idea what this means? She's... she's..." but Rose couldn't finish the sentence. She yanked a large pink towel from the rack and dragged the young girl from the tub wrapping her in the towel.

"Oh Rose, calm yourself and tell me what you're talking about." Herb smiled reassuringly at his granddaughter, who continued to fight back the tears, the words of her beloved grandmother reverberating in her mind, "That's a bad girl."

Rose grabbed her husband's shoulder. Herb winced from the intensity of the grip. Rose bit her lower lip, the lipstick applied early that morning long ago worn away and tried again. "She's only seven, and it's already started. I was almost twelve before Satan tempted me, and Evelyn had just turned ten when the curse first visited her. Now, here's her daughter changing the course of her bath water with the flick of her finger. Oh, Lord, what are we going to do?"

Finding it oddly humorous, yet unaccustomed to seeing his wife so emotionally distraught, Herb tried to keep from smiling knowing it would be like trying to put out a candle flame by pouring gasoline on it. He gently took Amberlin from Rose's arms, as he replied, "Well, to start with, we won't panic. We don't know if Amberlin is exhibiting special talents or not."

"But I saw it. The water was turning in its proper direction as God intended, then she waved her finger and reversed the flow. Water all over the world flows either clockwise or counter-clockwise, Herb, depending on which side of the equator you're talking about. That's the way God intended it to be."

Allowing himself just the hint of a smile, Herb gently rocked Amberlin to calm her as he caressed her golden curls still wet from the shampooing. "Well, it's a bit of an old wives...uh, a misconception to think that all whirlpools turn in the same direction. I wrote an article a few years ago on why cyclones rotate clockwise in the southern hemisphere and counterclockwise in the northern. I found out during my research it's due to the inertial force of the rotating Earth, but it takes a tremendous amount of air or water for it to take effect. For smaller amounts, like the water in Amberlin's tub, there are many factors that could have influenced the direction including the shape of the container it's in, other currents, etc. Who knows? She could have been moving her toes in the water creating a new current affecting the water's direction. That would hardly take God's or Satan's intervention."

The logic quieted Rose, probably more from confusion than understanding.

"Now, go get ready for bed, and I'll tuck Amberlin in. It's all going to be okay." Herb shared another reassuring smile with both of them. Only Amberlin smiled back.

"Yea, I'm glad you're gonna tuck me in," she said. Placing her head on his shoulder, she tried unsuccessfully to stifle a yawn.

"That's right, dear heart. It'll be my pleasure."

"TOP BUNK OR BOTTOM bunk, tonight?" Herb asked as he entered Amberlin's room even though he knew the answer.

"Bottom, please. The top is too high," Amberlin replied. As he lowered her into bed, she asked, "Will you tell me a story, Papa Herb? One of your real ones?"

He sat on the bed next to her and chuckled. How she loved his stories, especially the "real" ones about his life growing up with at least a thread of truth in them. He paused, trying to think of one he hadn't told her recently.

"How about the time I met a real spiritual sage?"

"Sure," Amberlin replied, then, "What's a spirit sage?"

"Spiritual sage," Herb corrected her, "is someone who has devoted their life to seeking a closer relationship with God, and who often shares their spiritual journey with others."

"What was the spiritual sage's name?" Amberlin asked as she snuggled down in her bed under her mother's childhood quilt preparing for the story.

"His name was Mo Zoloff, and I met him not too far from here in a retreat center outside of Black Mountain."

"I know where that is... kinda," Amberlin said.

"Yes, well, it's only about an hour or so drive from here, but when I first went there I was staying even closer at my family's summer cabin just outside of Black Mountain. It was the summer after I graduated from high school. I wasn't really a freelance writer yet, but I sure thought I was, or at least I knew that's what I wanted to be."

"How did you meet Mo?" Amberlin asked.

"Well, like I said, I heard him speak at this retreat center. I remember it like it was yesterday even though it was, well let's see, over thirty years ago."

"That's a long time, Papa Herb."

"Not really, sweetheart. It's just a blink of God's eye," Herb replied. Closing his own eyes, he could picture the rustic assembly hall filled with people awaiting the start of Master Mo's talk. "I remember it like it was yesterday," he repeated with his eyes still closed.

I sat about four rows from the back. I could have sat closer, but I felt out of my element. This was my first time to be in the presence of an actual guru from India, at least that was who I thought Master Mo was at the time. You can imagine my surprise when a short, slim white man in his mid- to late-thirties wearing a white t-shirt and black baggie pants strolled onto the stage to a sturdy table sitting in the middle. He stepped out of his sandals and climbed onto the table where he sat cross-legged facing the audience. The room had filled to about three-fourths full, but Mo continued to sit there with his eyes closed. Meditating, I guess.

"What's that?" asked Amberlin.

"Meditating is kinda like prayer except, instead of talking to God, you're listening for God to talk to you," replied Papa Herb.

"Oh!" whispered Amberlin in awe.

As the room filled, he continued to sit quietly, apparently lost in his thoughts. The minutes dragged by, as I began to fidget in my chair along with a number of other people. Then we all grew quiet again in anticipation of Master Mo's talk.

Finally the figure in the center of the stage opened his eyes and gazed around for a moment, a smile growing on his face before he finally broke the silence.

"I'm thrilled to see so many people gather here for a two-hour silent meditation," Mo said.

There was a moment of shocked silence as everyone glanced at each other before realizing it was a joke. Then the whole audience burst out laughing as Master Mo joined them. As the laughter finally died down, he spoke again.

"And so... we begin."

And so we did. For the next hour, I sat mesmerized by the quiet man with the deeply moving and inspiring message. He challenged the audience to look within themselves for their spark of divinity. He accused our Western culture of looking too much to the East to places like India and Tibet for our spiritual sages. He suggested it was time for us in the Western hemisphere to create our own spiritual leaders. He even went so far as to suggest there could be a spiritual sage sitting right there in our own seat.

I was so moved by his message by the end of the talk I overcame my usual shyness and approached him on the stage, along with a number of other enthusiastic people. When my turn came, I handed Mo my business card. I had them printed the week before with my name and phone number and under my name the bold declaration, Writer.

"I'd like to help you share your message with more people," I stammered. I was so shy I could hardly speak.

Mo smiled knowingly, nodding his head. "Come see me tomorrow – noontime. Don't be late."

I nodded in return. I wasn't sure how I was going to get myself back the next day, but I knew I would, and I did. In fact, I was back at the retreat center before 11 o'clock, which was a good thing because I had failed to ask Mo where we would meet. It took me close to an hour to find out he was staying in one of the dorm rooms just like everyone else, although he wasn't sharing it with anyone like most of the retreat participants.

I knocked lightly on the door, wondering what in the world I was doing there. Then I heard Mo's calm, soothing voice telling me to enter. Taking a deep breath and squaring my shoulders like my father had taught me, I turned the handle and walked in.

Mo sat at one of the desks scribbling in a notebook. Hearing me enter, he looked up from his work and smiled warmly.

"Ahh, my young writer friend who is going to make me famous by sharing my message with the rest of the world. Come in my friend. Make yourself comfortable," he said pointing to a nearby chair.

As I sat down, I gazed around and realized the only light in the room, other than what was filtering in from the window, came from a dozen or so candles distributed throughout the room.

"I was capturing some thoughts from my meditation," Mo explained, noticing my puzzled look. "We can turn on some lights if you prefer."

"No, this is fine," I replied, trying to hide my nervousness. "I appreciate you taking time to see me."

"Oh, my pleasure. I'm intrigued to meet a young writer with such an aura of destiny surrounding him." As he said this, Mo stood up from the desk and walked over to the nearby bed to sit cross-legged.

"First, let's address the reason you thought you were coming to see me—your interest in writing about me. When I return to my ashram, I will have someone send you background information about my work. Upon reviewing it, if you need additional information including an interview, I'll be happy to oblige. Will that work for you?"

"What's an ash room?" Amberlin asked.

Herb was momentarily startled as he remembered he was sharing his story with his granddaughter.

"It's ashram, sweetie. It's a spiritual community, not too different from our community here." Amberlin nodded, apparently satisfied with his answer so he continued.

"Yes sir," I almost shouted. "That would be great." Mustering up my courage, I continued, "What do you mean, the reason you thought you were coming here? Why do you think I'm really here?"

Mo only smiled at first, nodding his head. "So I can confirm for myself what I felt when we first met was indeed true, and if true, I could share it with you."

"And what was that?"

"Your divine destiny," Mo replied.

"My what?"

"Your divine destiny," Mo repeated. "You can think of it as a little like fate—a future inevitable event or events—but one that's divinely guided. Of course, that might be a bit overstated. We do continue to exercise free choice and free will, so nothing is completely inevitable, although yours might be as close to inevitable as I've ever seen."

I could feel the hairs on the back of my neck stand at attention as Mo spoke. I wasn't too sure I wanted to know my divine destiny, but then again, how could I refuse? After all, as a seventeen-years-old, I could use as much help with my future as the next recently graduated high school student.

Mo said, "Pull your chair over next to the bed. Don't worry. I won't bite. I just need to make a stronger connection."

I did as he instructed. Funny, looking back on it now, I should have been more concerned about what this strange little man might do to me, but for some reason I wasn't afraid at all. I was mostly concerned he might tell me my divine destiny was to be a failure, failing at everything I tried.

I sat there in my chair, just a foot or two from where Mo sat on the bed. He instructed me to close my eyes and to take several deep breaths. Around the third or fourth breath, I felt a light pressure on either side of my forehead and realized it was Mo's fingers lightly touching my temples. They stayed there, just barely perceptible. I started to open my eyes, and then thought better of it.

After what felt like a minute or two, I heard a voice. It didn't sound like Mo, but it must have been since there wasn't anyone else in the room. The voice was about an octave lower than Mo's and with a strong, foreign accent I hadn't heard before or since.

"What did he say, Papa Herb?" Amberlin's sleepy voice brought Herb back to the present, but he continued in silence for a moment before answering.

"Well, sweetie, he told me I was destined to be a protector and preparer—someone who would prepare the way. That's what he said."

"A protector and preparer for what?"

"He didn't exactly say, but he did tell me I would know at the right time," Herb replied, grasping Amberlin's hand that had snuck out from under the covers.

"And did you?"

Herb pondered the question for a moment before replying.

"I guess I can best answer your question this way. I believe God sometimes gives us a second chance to fulfill our destiny, and I certainly feel like he's given me a second chance to fulfill mine." He paused again, unsure whether to continue, and then added. "I feel like you're my second chance. I'm here to protect you and to prepare you so you can fulfill your destiny."

He wasn't sure whether Amberlin had heard his last comment. Her eyes were closed, and her breathing was slow and shallow. When he turned to cut off the light next to her bed, he heard her whisper, "Papa Herb's my protector and provider." She sighed as she turned on her side and snuggled deeper under the covers.

Herb leaned over and kissed her on the forehead. "That's right, sweetheart. As long as there's breath left in this body, I'll always be here for you. I won't make the same mistake twice." He straightened the covers, then turned and tiptoed from the room. As he gently closed the door to Amberlin's room, he remembered leaving Mo's room over thirty years ago.

His hand had been on the door of Mo's room when the question suddenly occurred to him. "Master Mo, could I ask you one last question?"

"What is it, son?"

"Well, it seems that, often, spiritual matters come in threes, you know, like the Holy Trinity. I was just wondering if there's a third word to go along with protect and prepare?"

Mo considered the question then smiled. "Yes, you could say there is. It's 'purpose.' The one you will protect and prepare will bring purpose to the world. Go in peace, Herb."

As Herb reached Rose and his bedroom, he braced himself for what he might face on the other side of the bedroom door, but as he entered the room he breathed a sigh of relief. Rose was already asleep.

He quietly changed into his pajamas and walked over to Rose's side of the bed to kiss her goodnight. As he bent over her, he paused and gazed at her wrinkled face covered with cold cream, oh so familiar, after close to thirty years of marriage. He realized now when he took the vow to prepare and protect Amberlin; it might include protecting his granddaughter from his wife and the rest of the community where Rose was such an important member. The task that lay before him loomed much larger than he had at first imagined--much larger and much more important too.

CHAPTER TWO
Homeschooled

IT'S CHOICE - NOT CHANCE - that determines your destiny. Jean Nidetch

Herb awoke the next morning to the smell of bacon and the phrase "protect and prepare" reverberating around in his head. He wasn't sure whether Amberlin had changed the direction of the whirlpool the night before but he was pretty sure his explanation to Rose though true, hadn't convinced her of her granddaughter's innocence.

After all, she'd been looking for some signs of Satan appearing in Amberlin, and Herb knew if you looked long enough for something you were bound to find it sooner or later. In Rose's case, it had been sooner.

As he dressed and prepared himself for the day, he was already strategizing how to fulfill his mission. "Not going to make the same mistake twice," he muttered as he walked downstairs. It was rapidly becoming his mantra.

"Hello, my dear hearts. How are my two lovely ladies this fine morning?"

Rose glanced over at him from where she stood in front of the stove watching over the bacon. "My, aren't you a happy fella this morning?" she asked, but in a lighthearted voice that meant she also was in a better frame of mind.

"Morning, Papa Herb," Amberlin said from where she sat at the table, holding her arms out to him for a hug, which he happily obliged her with.

Rose brought the platter of eggs and bacons over to the table. "Toast will be ready in a minute." If she even remembered last night's incident she gave no hint of it, but that was just like her. Being a Southern lady, if there's one thing she'd learned from childhood, it was what Herb called "Southern nice." He'd heard other people, especially transplanted Northerners, refer to as covert.

As a Southern gentleman, Herb knew how to play this chess game. He waited as breakfast got under way, the blessing was said, and most of breakfast eaten before he moved his center pawn forward.

"Do you have a busy day today, Rose?" He asked between mouthfuls of eggs and grits.

"Why you know I do, Herb. At ten o'clock I have a meeting with the Community Board to discuss plans for our next quarter, and that's just the start of my day. Seems like the older I get, the more responsibilities I'm expected to fulfill. I don't know how Golden Acres would get along if something were to happen to me."

"I wonder if your great-great granddaddy had any idea how much this community would grow when he donated the land?"

"Bless his heart, I doubt it, but it sure did seal my fate without him ever even knowing me," Rose replied. As the sole-surviving member of the Drayton family who had bestowed the land for the Golden Acres of Christ Community, being busy was her favorite complaint. Herb decided it was time to move his next chess piece into action.

"Well, I've been thinking about how busy you are and all. You know I'm not much when it comes to Community matters," one of the largest understatements of the year. Rose and he had come to an agreement over two decades ago. He would put in the necessary appearances to keep the rumor mill off their back, as long as Rose gave him the room and the privacy to pursue his interests without interruption or interference. Although, like Rose, Herb had been born and raised in the Followers of Christ Assembly Church, his values and beliefs had evolved but not before falling madly in love with Rose. The agreement had, no doubt, saved their marriage.

"So, I've been wondering how I could help out a bit, and it came to mind you have so much to do to keep this community running..." Here goes, a bold move of his knight into the center of the board.

"I'd like to offer to help out by taking a more active role in Amberlin's homeschooling. Could you pass the grits, sweetheart?" Rose had insisted Amberlin be taught at home because it was the best way to assure she received a good Christian education. Her reasoning hadn't fooled Herb. He knew it was her deep fear that Amberlin might be visited by Satan while in school, condemning the entire family to another round of malicious gossip. That would certainly ruin them, and possibly lead to expulsion from the community.

He made it a point not to stare at Rose, but instead kept his wife in the corner of his eye as she pondered his offer while passing the grits.

"That's very thoughtful of you, Herb. I must confess Amberlin's education has been taking a backseat of late. I suppose I could use some help."

"Well, I can sure understand that Rose dear, with all the other important matters you have on your mind. You know, I've always thought I might have missed my calling by not becoming a teacher, and this way it might not be too late to answer God's call." There, he'd moved his Queen off the back line where she could do some good; that is if Rose didn't counterattack.

"Papa Herb? You want to be my teacher?" Amberlin spoke up, surprising both of them.

"Why sugar, I didn't have any idea you were following this conversation." Rose reached over and patted Amberlin's hand lightly. Herb noticed the hand was still red from where Rose had slapped it so roughly the night before but didn't say anything.

"Would you like your Papa Herb to be your teacher?"

"Really?" Amberlin replied then nodding her head vigorously. "That would be great."

"Well, I guess that settles it," Rose said, as Herb breathed a quiet sigh of relief. "At least on a trial basis," Rose added.

"Sure, exactly. We'll give it a try and see how it works out." But Herb knew the agreement had been sealed. Rose would be too busy with her many other Community duties to monitor any trial run.

"Not going to make the same mistake twice," he muttered for the second time this morning.

"What was that, dear?"

"Nothing," Herb replied as he stood up. "Let me take care of the dishes. You go ahead and get ready for your meeting."

After Rose had left to dress for her day, Herb began to clean up.

"Can I help?" his granddaughter asked, as she slid off her chair.

"Sure, you can help, just be careful not to drop anything," Herb replied, as he scraped the last of the grits into a bowl. "We'll take these out to Ruffin in a few minutes. He's a good Southern dog that never turns down a bowl of grits." He handed Amberlin a dry dishtowel.

"You can dry the dishes, but be very careful. Wet dishes can be slippery and end up making a big mess on the floor if you drop one."

"I'll be careful, Papa Herb," she said as she took the first dish from the dish rack where Herb had placed it.

"Speaking of being careful, I want to talk to you about last night," Herb said. He paused before going on to make sure Rose wasn't within earshot.

"I'm sorry, Papa Herb. I didn't mean to be a bad girl."

Herb took another towel from where they hung on the oven door and dried his hands. Bending down to Amberlin's height, he gently grasped her shoulders and looked straight into her blue-green eyes. "Sweetheart, that's what I want to talk to you about. What you did, whatever it was and however you did it, wasn't wrong. Your grandmother made a mistake. It was late, and she was tired... and scared."

"Grandma scared? What could I do to scare her, Papa Herb?"

"Many people become scared about things they don't understand, your grandmother included. There are things about you that are a mystery, but that doesn't make them wrong or bad. However, I think it would be a good idea if we didn't frighten Rose or the others in the Community. Don't you agree?"

Amberlin thought about this a moment, a confused look on her young face. After a moment, she asked, "But what is it that frightens them?"

"Humm, that's a good question," Herb replied. Of course, how would Amberlin know what special powers she might have that others didn't. "Tell you what. That will be our first lesson. Right after breakfast, we'll go out to the Sanctuary."

"Where, Papa Herb?"

"Oh, that's the name I've given to my office space out back, and now it's the name you and I can call it, but only when no one else is around. We'll go over some of the things that frighten others so you'll know what not to do in front of them. Okay?"

Amberlin smiled and giggled. "First lesson in the Saint-u-airy."

After finishing the dishes, Herb and Amberlin walked along the gravel path to the small cottage about twenty yards from the main house. It was once a guesthouse, but after Herb and Rose had made their agreement, Herb had taken it over as his office space. It wasn't long before he thought of it as his sanctuary away from the craziness of the world, and the name stuck.

As they approached the cottage, Ruffin stuck his head out from his doghouse and took a sniff of the air. "He smells those grits you have, Amberlin. Better let him have them."

As Amberlin put the bowl down, the blue-merle, rough-coated Australian Sheepdog pulled himself from his shelter, stretched his front legs, then his back ones before moving in on the bowl of grits.

"Ruffin likes grits," Amberlin said as she rubbed the soft fur behind Ruffin's ears.

"That's for sure," Herb said with a laugh. "Unfortunately, they go straight to his hips. I might need you to start walking him around the neighborhood to take off some of that weight. Come to think of it, I might need to join the two of you on those walks." He patted his less than flat stomach then reached down and undid the chain from Ruffin's collar.

"When you finish your breakfast, you can come to the office," Herb said to his aging companion. Ruffin was rarely allowed in the main house. Rose felt that if God had intended dogs to be indoors, he wouldn't have designed their coats to shed, but Ruffin seemed content to make the Sanctuary his home.

The layout of the Sanctuary was one large living area that included a kitchenette, a smaller bedroom, and a bathroom. Herb had converted the living area into his office and library, leaving the bedroom to collect clutter through the years.

"We'll clean out the back room and convert it into your school room. How will that be?" Herb asked as he turned on the lights, and breathed a deep sigh as he gazed around the cozy room. He truly felt more at home in this one room than he did anywhere in the main house.

"I'm happy you are going to be my teacher," Amberlin said again.

"That's right. I can't think of a better way to prepare and protect you."

"Prepare me for what? Protect me from what?" Amberlin asked as she climbed onto the overstuffed couch setting against one wall across from the stone fireplace.

"Well, answering those two questions is the perfect place to start, I guess." Herb pulled the swivel chair from his desk and pushed it closer to the sofa.

"Humm, let's see, where to begin?" He paused for a moment, rubbing the coarse whiskers on his chin. "I'm not completely sure what I'm to prepare you for, least not yet, except... I'd say for starters, to prepare you for life, and for your destiny."

"What is a destiny, Papa Herb?"

Herb smiled. Homeschooling his precocious granddaughter wasn't going to be as easy as he'd thought. "I believe the Creator has placed each one of us here on Earth for a special reason. Some people call it a life purpose, others call it their destiny. It means we're each here for a reason, and I believe you're here for a particularly special reason, although I have to admit, I don't know what it is yet."

"Then how are you going to prepare me for it?" Amberlin asked with a coy smile on her face.

"Well dear, that's another good question. I thought I'd be the one asking you the tough questions," Herb said. "Remember what Mo told me just before I left his room, when I asked him about the third word?"

Amberlin frowned for a moment, trying to remember. "I was just about asleep by then."

"Well, he said the third word was "purpose," and that the person who I was to prepare and protect would bring a deeper sense of purpose to Earth. So that's where we'll begin. In fact, I'd say we already have."

Apparently satisfied with that answer, Amberlin nodded. "And what are you to protect me from?"

"Anything and anybody who would keep you from fulfilling your life purpose," Herb replied without hesitation.

"Who would do that?" Amberlin asked, a concerned look starting to appear on her face.

"Oh, plenty of folks, I'm afraid, mostly out of ignorance and fear." Herb paused trying to think of a simple way to share his thoughts with his granddaughter. Finally, he continued. "What I'm about to share with you, you might not understand, least not all of it, but we'll continue to talk about it from time to time until you do. Okay?"

"Sure, Papa Herb. I'll try my best."

"That's good, sweetheart. So will I. Let's see...where to begin? There are different ways we can know God. I won't go into all of them right now, but one of the ways is to think of God as our protector. I know you've heard the stories in Sunday school about God being up in heaven looking down over us to keep us safe, right?"

"Yes, they tell us about him watching over us all the time."

"That's one way to know God. If we're in trouble, he's there to watch over us and protect us. Have they also spoken to you about God giving Moses the Ten Commandments?"

"Yea, sure," Amberlin replied, "but I don't remember all of them, but don't tell grandma."

Papa Herb chuckled. "That's okay, sweetheart. We'll keep these lessons between you and me. Besides, you'll have plenty of time to learn the Commandments over and over, I'm sure."

"Where was I? Oh yes...another way to think of God is like the Supreme Rule Maker. And if we think of God as our protector, like a parent, as well as someone who gives us certain rules to follow, what should we as good children do?"

"Follow the rules and do what he says!" Amberlin replied quickly.

"Exactly," Herb chuckled. "Those are two important and common ways for us, his children, to know God. Is this making sense?"

"Yes, I think so," Amberlin answered. "But what does this have to do with people being stupid and afraid?"

"Well, dear, I didn't say they were stupid," Herb tried to suppress his grin. "Stupid means someone isn't willing to learn or can't learn. Ignorance is when someone isn't informed. They just don't know any better."

"But that's another good question. You see, sometimes people get stuck knowing God in only those two ways. They never bother to look further or to consider other ways to connect with God. When that happens, and unfortunately it has happened a lot throughout history, people often become afraid when God shows up in different ways. They may think that their way of knowing God is the only way. That's their ignorance showing, and when God shows up in different ways or when other people get to know God in different ways, it frightens them."

"But what other ways are there to know God?" Amberlin asked, a perplexed look on her face.

"Well, as I said, there are many different ways, more than I've discovered at this point in my life. Let me share another way by telling you a story about your grandmother Rose. I think you'll begin to understand why she was frightened by what she saw last night.

"The story takes place many years ago, when Rose was a young girl, not too much older than you. I didn't know her then, but she told me this story once before we were married because she was afraid if I found out on my own I wouldn't want to stay married to her. The incident happened in this community, and while almost no one knows about it, Rose was still afraid I might find out from someone else.

"The voices, as Rose calls them, started when she was twelve. She began to know things about the people around her—things they hadn't told her. At first, she didn't think much about it assuming everyone else had the same ability. Before long she figured out she knew things in ways that others didn't. She finally shared this with her best friend, Missy."

"Missy Stover, the reverend's wife?"

"Yes, except her name was Missy McMillan at the time, and this was long before Reverend Stover. Missy and Rose grew up together as best friends. When Missy found out about this inner knowing your grandmother had, she didn't believe it at first, so she challenged her to put it to a test."

"A test?" Amberlin asked.

"Yes, an experiment to see how accurate it was and to see if it was real. There was another little girl in their class named Emily Rogers that neither of them liked, but Missy particularly disliked her. Missy asked Rose to see if the voices could tell her what Emily's greatest fears were. It took a few weeks for Rose to come up with the answer since this ability was new, and she was still learning about it. But one night her voices told her Emily was deathly afraid of two things, spiders and the dark."

"Emily sounds a lot like me," Amberlin said. "I'm not too crazy about either one of those."

"It was even worse for Emily. She had what is known as a phobia against spiders and also about being in the dark. In fact, it was so bad her parents kept a small lamp in the shape of an angel turned on in her room even when she slept. Also, she was constantly asking her parents to check under her bed for spiders.

"When Missy learned of this, she decided the only way to check to be sure the information was true was to put it to a test."

"How'd they do that?" Amberlin asked.

"Late one night after everyone had gone to bed, Rose and Missy met outside Emily's home. Over the last few days, they had collected a jar full of spiders from every dark little hole they could find. Missy climbed into Emily's bedroom with the spiders and one other surprise for Emily while Rose entered the basement where the fuse box was.

"Fuse box? What's that?"

"It's what controls the electricity through the house. By loosening a fuse, you can cut the power to that section of the house."

"Oh," Amberlin said. Then realizing what that meant, she repeated, "Oh, I see."

"As soon as the nightlight went off in Emily's room, Missy dumped the spiders out on Emily's bed and replaced the nightlight she had left over from Halloween in the shape of a spider. Just before climbing out the window, she shook Emily awake."

"What happened?" Amberlin asked.

"Unfortunately the test proved beyond a shadow of a doubt Emily hated spiders and the dark more than anything in the world. They kept her in the dark for several minutes with the spiders climbing over her bed and on her. Then Rose replaced the fuse turning the spider light on. That's when Emily started screaming. The combination of darkness and spiders was too much for her. She flew into hysterics, crying and screaming, and swatting at the spiders climbing over her. Finally in a blind panic, she ran out of the room, down the hallway, tripped at the top of the stairs and fell."

Amberlin gasped.

"Seeing what happened, Missy quickly climbed back in the room, exchanged the night lights, and escaped out the window.

"What happened to Emily?"

"They said she was dead before she reached the bottom of the stairs from a broken neck."

"Oh, no." Amberlin gasped. "Poor Emily."

"Yep. No one ever quite understood what made her panic. They figured it was probably a bad dream. Of course, Rose and Missy knew. That's when Rose decided the 'voices' inside her were a curse from Satan. She refused to listen to them or ever talk about them again with Missy or anyone else."

"Wow!" Amberlin said, with eyes shining bright with amazement. "No wonder she's afraid. Is Satan tempting me too, Papa Herb?"

"No sweetie. That's what Rose is afraid might be happening," Papa Herb replied, "but I have a different opinion. Do you want to hear it?"

"Sure. After all, you're my teacher here to prepare and protect me." Amberlin smiled revealing her two charming dimples.

Herb smiled back. "I think these special powers the women of this family have are like other gifts and talents we all have. I have the talent of writing; others have the talent of being able to draw well while other people have musical talents. In other words, God has given us all special gifts. Some gifts are more common and are for this reason considered more acceptable. Others, like yours and Rose's are...well, less common."

Papa Herb leaned in closer to Amberlin. "It's what we do with our talents that determine whether they are truly gifts or curses. You see, Missy convinced your grandmother to use her gift in an evil and malicious way so they became a curse."

Amberlin thought hard about what Papa Herb said and decided it made sense to her. "So there's nothing wrong with what I can do as long as I don't use my gifts to do wrong things?"

"Exactly, sweetheart. Rather than rejecting or denying your special gifts from God, embrace them, develop them with the intention to do good and do so carefully."

"Why's that?"

"Because remember, not everyone has the same way of viewing them as you and I do. I'm afraid people in the Golden Acres Community spend much of their time stuck in fear. Anything that is different or they don't understand, like your special powers, is automatically assumed to be trouble."

"And from the devil," Amberlin added.

"That's right," Papa Herb sighed. "If you notice new things that you can do that you're not sure others can do..."

"Like moving the water around?" Amberlin asked.

"Like moving the water around," Herb agreed. "Or hearing voices, having a feeling you know what's going to happen before it does, or knowing what someone else is thinking without them telling you..."

"Wow! I'll be able to do all that?"

Papa Herb chuckled. "I don't know sweetheart. I just don't know. Only God knows at this point what you'll be capable of as you grow older." As Papa Herb gave it more thought, he had a feeling she might have more power than either of them could imagine.

"I do know this though. You're here for a very special reason. In truth, we all are. I just have a hunch your reason may be even more special."

Amberlin thought about her grandfather's words. "Papa Herb, is a 'hunch' one of those special gifts from God?"

Herb laughed again. "Could be. It sure could be." He patted her lightly on the head then a thought came to him. "You know, now that you mention it, having hunches and inner voices and the like could be considered another way of knowing God. It's called the 'intuitive response,' and we all have the ability whether we develop it or not. The potential to tap into God's wisdom in this way exists within us all. Unfortunately in Rose's world she couldn't be open to that possibility, but you can."

Amberlin sat quietly, nodding her head with a faraway look of innocence in her eye. "Okay, let's not blow a fuse in your brain on our very first day. How about you and I turn that junk room in yonder into your special class-room?"

"Yea!" Amberlin shouted. "I like having you as my teacher."

CHAPTER THREE
The Asylum

GOOD is good and bad is bad, and nowhere is the difference between good and bad so wide and so fateful as in human character. For character makes destiny in the individual and in the race. Edward O. Sisson

FIVE YEARS LATER 1957

From the road, most people who drove by might have though the sprawling building was simply one of the many lodges nestled throughout the Blue Ridge Mountains, but their assessment would be several decades out of date. Since the administration of the Asylum preferred maintaining a low profile, the rhododendrons had been encouraged to grow over the sign. Behind the lodge hidden from view from the road were four utilitarian looking buildings. These were the medical wings where the patients were housed. Behind those, recessed even deeper in the woods, stood wing number five. The few people who knew of its existence called it the Madden Wing in commemoration of Reverend Charles Madden who had donated the money for its construction.

Since most strangers thought they'd passed another lodge more run down than the others in the area, they seldom bothered to stop. The locals knew it was the local mental asylum. Almost no one knew it was also a prison where the Followers of Christ sequestered their mentally ill, their dissidents and the occasional Fallen Follower whose soul had been lost to Satan. No one in the area called it by its official name: Western Carolina Sanitarium. It was simply the Asylum.

Miriam Mason came to the quiet mountain village of Foster Flats just a few miles from Black Mountain with the insights of a local. After all, Foster Flats had been her home for the first seventeen years of her life and her mom's home for over sixty years. Still, Miriam was surprised to find herself back in Foster Flats. Her life had been going according to plan until it had taken a sudden sharp and unpredictable twist from which she was still reeling. She'd graduated with honors from Woodruff School of Nursing as one of the youngest in her class. On top of that, during her senior year she met and married the man of her dreams Eric Mason, an up-and-coming enlisted man. Within a year, she was pregnant with Matty. His full name was Matthew, but such a tiny, precious bundle of God's spirit wasn't quite ready for such a long name.

They were living just off the Army base at Camp Lejeune where Eric was in training when Miriam's life path took the sharp hairpin turn. The officers delivered the letter at 3:33 pm on March third. From that moment, Miriam developed a passionate dislike for the number three. The short letter, written on crisp white paper with the official letterhead of the commanding officer, informed her Sergeant Eric Mason had been killed in a freak accident during a training maneuver.

Suddenly, Miriam found herself with a newborn baby in a harsh military town with few friends and little support. Just when she felt life couldn't get any worse a second letter arrived, this one from Alice Grissom, her mother's longtime next-door neighbor informing her that Mama Winslow had suffered a minor stroke. It took Miriam only three days to pack up her belongings into a U-Haul truck. She headed home to Foster Flat with Matty beside her, a steady stream of tears leaking from her brown eyes and muttering a prayer to God for guidance.

She hoped that between her government check and her mother's social security they'd be able to make it financially. Unfortunately, Mama Winslow's medical bills kept climbing, so as her mother slowly recovered from the stroke, Miriam looked for a job where she could use her nurse's training. However, in such a small town, the choices were limited. In fact, the only real choice was Western Carolina Sanitarium, or as the locals called it, the Asylum. Miriam had been reluctant to turn over Matty's care to her partially invalid mother, but Mama Winslow assured her she could look after him just fine.

"I'm sure Matty and I will get along. What a perfect way for me to get to know my grandson. Besides, if I need help, Alice is just next door. Shoot, nowadays she spends as much time over here as she does at her house. She calls this her home away from home. Remember, we Christians need to stay flexible, 'cause we never know where God might need us. You just go talk to that Dr. Allen. You'll know whether that's where you're meant to be God's servant next."

It was one of her favorite sayings Miriam had grown up with though lately she felt sore from all the stretching God had been putting her through. But she'd learned long ago that it was a waste of time to argue with her mom when she'd made up her mind. By the set of Mama Winslow's chin, it was clear her mind was made. So Miriam accepted the position at the Asylum, even though the pay was far below what she should have been able to receive, given her training and experience. But the administrator, Dr. Nick Allen, had been a much better negotiator than Miriam. He knew about her mother's condition and Matty, and he knew the limited opportunities for a nurse in the area.

Dr. Allen looked over her resume through tired, weepy eyes. Miriam thought he looked like he was about to cry but then realized it was his normal appearance, due in large part to the long hours and many headaches that came with his job. When she remarked how low the starting salary was, he replied, "Yes, I know. Times are tough all over, and that's certainly true for our humble facilities here. Look at it this way. When you consider the next closest facility you might find a job is all the way in Asheville, and by the time you take in the commute time and expense, will you really be doing any better? Besides, the patients in the Madden Wing could benefit from your care."

It was the last statement that sealed the deal. Maybe her mom was right. The Lord did work in mysterious ways. Maybe He was guiding her back home, not only to help her mother and her son, but also to serve a greater purpose with the patients who called the Madden Wing home.

"May I see where I'll be working, Dr. Allen?"

"Sure you may, Nurse Mason...on Monday when you start work," Dr. Allen quickly replied as he slid the contract in front of her. Noticing her shocked appearance, he continued. "We have an exterminator in there at the moment, so it's really not a good time for a tour. Now, if you'll just sign these papers, we'll get you on the payroll."

And so it began. The following Monday, she met the day nurse, Miss Rachel Rankin, a middle-aged woman with salt and pepper hair tied back in a tight bun. Miriam thought it must give her a constant headache along with a mild slanting of her eyes. During their first meeting, Nurse Ranking laid down the law. To say that Nurse Rankin's demeanor towards Miriam was cold would be an understatement. No sooner had Miriam sat down in the straight back oak chair, eliciting a grating creak from its joints, than Nurse Rankin looked over her reading glasses at Miriam with a frown and shake of her head.

"Let's get one thing straight, right from the start, Nurse Mason. We currently have twelve patients here in the Madden Wing. We had twelve patients a year ago; we're likely to have the same twelve patients a year from today. We have room for four more patients though I don't expect any others at present. In other words, these are chronic care patients. There's little hope of their recovery. They don't expect it, their families don't expect, and it'll be a lot easier for you if you don't expect it. Our job is to keep them reasonably comfortable, keep them from hurting themselves or each other, and keep them out of trouble until the good Lord decides to take them home. Is that clear?"

A whirl of responses spun around in Miriam's head, but before she could decide whether to articulate any of them, Nurse Rankin continued.

"We have two orderlies that work in the Madden Wing. Part of their compensation is room and board, so at least one of them should always be available to you. Their names are Jeremy Knight and Isaac Irons. Jeremy is a Negro, but he knows his place. Neither of them is particularly bright, but both are strong and will follow orders if you stay on them. Don't coddle them, Nurse Mason. It's taken me over a year to put the fear of God in them, and I don't need some wet-behind-the-ears nurse ruining my hard work. Do you understand?"

Miriam opened her mouth to ask a question, but before she could get it out, Nurse Rankin continued on her roll. "In just a minute I'll walk you through the ward and give you a brief rundown on the patients. They're still restrained in their rooms, and I'm sure they're not too happy about it. I nor-mally let them out around 7:30 after I've had a cup of coffee, but I knew you'd be coming in so I didn't bother. Ready?" Rankin stood up and walked out of the room without waiting for a reply. Miriam took a deep breath, said a silent prayer for patience and understanding, and followed her.

The two nurses walked down the hall towards the entrance to the Madden Wing. The walls were painted utilitarian gray with the standard black and white checked linoleum floor. No expense had been spared to make the Madden Wing look as sparse and unappealing as possible. The entrance was marked by an oak desk, a duplicate of the one in Nurse Rankin's office that looked like it had been donated by the local school system. In fact, all the furnishings looked like throwaways. Behind the desk was a black man dressed in green scrubs reading an outdated issue of National Geographic, which he quickly tossed onto the desk when he heard Nurse Rankin clear her throat.

"Jeremy, this is Nurse Mason, our new night nurse. You are to treat her with the same respect as me. If I hear otherwise, you'll answer to me. Is that clear?"

"Yes'um, Nurse Rankin. That's very clear. Don't have to worry about me none."

"How are the patients?"

"Fairly quiet. A few complained about not getting their breakfast on time. Nothing out of the ordinary."

"Okay. Make a note of the ones that complained and see that they get their breakfast last."

"Yes'um. Will do."

"Nurse Mason, come with me."

Nurse Rankin took a large set of keys from her pocket and unlocked the door that led into Madden Wing East.

"I'll give you a duplicate set of your own before you leave. Be sure to keep them on you at all times. Security is very important. Their limited freedom outside their rooms is a privilege, not a right. If anyone acts out, just let Jeremy or Isaac know, and they'll confine them. We also have a padded cell if anyone blows up. It's at the end of the hall." Rankin waved one arm in the general direction.

"Ahh, here we are. This is Birdman's nest...."

Golden Acres 1957

Herb gazed into the bathroom mirror as he straightened the narrow black tie, but his thoughts were far away. He had realized upon awakening this Sunday morning it had been five years since he'd offered to become Amberlin's teacher. As he had thought and hoped, Rose had never bothered to question the decision. It didn't hurt that his granddaughter was particularly smart and an easy student to teach. Teaching her had also become one of his greatest joys in life. It truly felt like a fulfillment of his purpose and destiny.

Of course, Amberlin had learned much more than her three R's under his tutelage. She'd also learned to be careful to hide her growing gifts and talents while becoming more comfortable with their unique qualities. Like her grandmother, Amberlin seemed to have the ability to discern things about people she met that she couldn't know any other way. Along with this, she appeared to be strongly empathic, also knowing how other people felt even when they tried to mask their emotions.

Herb suspected another gift may have begun to show itself. Over the past five years, Amberlin had spent many hours reading and studying in the Sanctuary with Ruffin lying next to her with his head in her lap as she stroked his mottled coat. At age eleven Ruffin showed signs of age, including a graying around his muzzle, but it seemed to Herb in other ways he had grown younger. His previously stiff limbs that had been particularly evident in the mornings seemed much more limber. His eyes appeared clearer with no evidence of the grayness of previous years that had suggested the start of cataracts. Perhaps I should start having Amberlin stroke my hair, Herb thought, as he brushed his own thinning but still thick white wavy hair.

Sundays were the highlight of the week for the Golden Acres Community. As one of its most prominent families, the Gentry's Sunday mornings started with an early breakfast before dressing up in their "Sunday Finest." Then they piled into Papa Herb's Buick to drive the short distance to Our Lord and Savior Church that served as the center hub of Golden Acres Community. Resting on the pinnacle of a knoll the church was one of the oldest structures in the area dating back to 1827 only a few years after the Gentry's manor was built. The church started out as a private chapel for the Gentry family. When Rose's great grandfather, Charles Gentry, donated the surrounding land to the Followers of Christ Assembly, he also deeded over the chapel, which was then expanded to become the worship center of the community.

The old church featured a high tower-like steeple and was surrounded by graves and headstones. Its dull gray slate shingles and stucco facade reminded Herb of a giant vulture standing guard over the decaying carcasses that surrounded it. The entire knoll was filled with gravestones of various shapes, sizes, and ages. It served as the burial grounds for many of the prominent families who had migrated to the community to worship in peace and later be buried in like fashion. It included the final resting place of several Confederate soldiers. The practice of burying the local community members wasn't limited to just the surrounding hillsides. It also included in the church itself, where some of the most prominent Followers of Christ had their mortal remains put to rest. Along much of the wall of the main sanctuary were ornate plaques with inscriptions like:

IN A VAULT BENEATH ARE DEPOSITED BESIDE HIS BELOVED
WIFE,
THE REMAINS OF CHARLES GARING
A NATIVE OF EXETER ENGLAND
DIED DECEMBER 7TH 1865, AGED 92

And:

IN LOVING MEMORY OF
HENRY IZARD MIDDLETON,
BORN JANUARY 27, 1881, DIED DECEMBER 9, 1952

Our Lord and Savior Church's architecture was a cross between a traditional Episcopal church and a Southern Baptist church. The main sanctuary was long and narrow with rows of pews, each with a place for hymnals on the back. The front of the church featured a tall pulpit where Reverend Stover stood each Sunday to deliver his scalding messages of fire and brimstone.

The church was the centerpiece of both worship and fellowship for the rest of Golden Acres Community members. But for Amberlin, as her powers continued to develop, the church became the focal point for disturbing feelings and emotions, making it increasingly difficult to enter the hallowed archway that led into the sanctuary.

She had always found the inner sanctum of the church less than inviting with its preponderance of dark wood and musty odor, mingled with the smell of furniture polish. But these emerging feelings were different, arising from deep within herself. She wondered if she was connecting with the residual spirits that surrounded the church? The sensations became increasingly difficult to tolerate. She found herself caught between the desire to be a good girl who did what she was told with the growing feelings of distress each time she even thought of entering the church.

When she mentioned these feelings to Papa Herb, he nodded quietly and patted her hand. Taking a deep breath, he said, "Your gifts seem be going through a growth spurt right now. It's a little like your body recently did when you were always hungry, and we couldn't seem to keep you filled. Do you remember that?"

Amberlin nodded. "But I'm not all that hungry these days."

"No," Papa Herb chuckled, "But you may start to be. We'll see. For sure, you're growing inside. The question is what to do about it. Rose will raise a huge ruckus if we tell her you can't attend church. She'd be sure the devil had possessed you in that case."

"We wouldn't want that," Amberlin said.

"That's for sure. I think it's time for you to begin to take control of your newly acquired talents, at least to the degree you can," Papa Herb continued.

"What does that mean?"

Papa Herb thought a moment before replying. "You know how you can close your eyes if there's something you don't want to see or cover your ears to keep from hearing something?"

"Yes," Amberlin said with a hint of uncertainty.

"This gives you some control over your senses. In the same way, I think you need to develop the ability to monitor what you allow into your psychic senses—not to deny or suppress them, but only to be more responsible for them. Does that make sense?"

"I guess so, Papa Herb, but how do I do that?"

"Boy, this is a little like the blind leading the blind here. I'm not sure how you're to do that since I don't have these special gifts myself, least not nearly to the degree you have. So, I suggest you play with them for a while. Each time you go near the church, for example, try different things to see what opens up your channel and what closes it down. You may not remember it now, but I imagine this is just what you did when you were a baby and were discovering how to see and hear."

Today would be the first time they'd visited the church since that conversation. Amberlin had mixed feelings about the trip. On the one hand, she was excited about the idea of playing with her growing gifts. At the same time, she wasn't looking forward to the uncomfortable sensations she knew she'd have to go through.

Sure enough, as they approached the center of the community, the troubling sensations started to grow. No time like the present to start playing, Amberlin thought as she first saw the church out of the car window. She closed her eyes and did feel a drop in the uncomfortable feelings. Next she covered her ears but found it made no difference. So, she sat in the back seat of the car with her eyes closed, trying to guess where they were along the drive to the church.

Then she discovered if she took her mind off the trip completely, thinking about something pleasant like playing with her dolls in her room or running with Ruffin outside, the discomfort almost completely left. So she quit trying to guess where they were and instead imagined she was back home playing in her room. She was surprised when Papa Herb announced they were at the church.

"All out who's getting out," Papa Herb said as he pulled up to the door. As with most of the older members of the church, Papa Herb had a habit of dropping Rose and Amberlin off at the door then driving down the hill to the parking area.

"Can I walk up with you, Papa Herb?" Amberlin asked; her eyes still closed.

"Why sure. I'd love the company, sweetheart, as long as you don't mind the walk."

Rose got out of the car. "Make sure you two aren't late. You know how I hate for any of us to be late. With our pew being up front, everyone notices."

"Don't worry, we'll be on time," Papa Herb assured her. "If need be, I'll carry Amberlin up on my shoulders."

After Rose had closed the door, and they started driving back down the road to the parking area, Papa Herb asked, "How are you doing, Sweetie?"

Amberlin explained what she'd learned so far.

"Interesting. You keep playing with it. I'm sure you'll be okay. Just take your time," Papa Herb said as they pulled into a parking space.

It was finally time. Amberlin could put it off no longer. She opened the car door, her eyes still closed. As her foot hit the pavement, a shockwave of emotion struck her in the solar plexus so hard her eyes flew open adding to the wave of nausea and...FEAR. That's what it was—a wave of fear that threatened to overpower her. It reminded her of a time at the beach about a year ago when an unexpectedly large wave had knocked her feet out from under her. It felt like that now; her knees felt like someone had suddenly struck them from behind. She stumbled for a moment before recovering her balance.

"Are you okay, sugar?" Papa Herb asked as he came around the corner of the car.

She closed her eyes for a moment and took a deep breath. Both seemed to help. She stood next to the car holding on to the door. "Yes, I think so."

I can do this. I can do this, she repeatedly thought as she took a second deep breath and slowly opened her eyes. A second wave of fear passed over her, but she was better prepared for this one, so it's wasn't as bad. It was working. She was learning to control the sensation. She braced herself, then looked up at Papa Herb, who was smiling down at her reassuringly. That helped. Slowly she turned to gaze up at the church allowing herself to take in first the graves then the steeple of the church, as she continued to breathe slowly and deeply. It was going to be a long morning.

CHAPTER FOUR
Hannah

THE Creator has not given you a longing to do what you have no ability to do.
Orison Swett Marden

"COME ON, HANNAH, OR we'll be late for church," Joseline Barrington shouted from the bathroom. She took a final look in the mirror to be sure her graying blonde hair wasn't too much of a rat's nest.

"What are you doing, anyway?" She asked, giving up on her hair and walking into the room that served both as her family's living and dining room.

"I'm giving Lucky a final brushing so he'll be pretty for church," eight-year-old Hannah replied from the single bedroom that the two of them shared.

"Well, Lucky can't go with us this time," her mother said from the door-way.

"I know he can't go in, but you've let him stay outside waiting on me before," Hannah said, her lower lip sticking out in an all-too-familiar pout.

"Well, he can't go this time because we're not going to our regular church. We're going to the large church on the hill."

"What?" Hannah gave Lucky a final pat then released him. It took both of them several seconds to stand up – Hannah because of the brace that forced her left leg to remain straight but also allowed her to walk; Lucky be-cause of a stiff rear leg left over from some long ago run-in with a car. "But all our friends and the people you work with are at the colored church."

"That may be true, but unlike them, we're white and we're allowed to attend the church of our choice, and today my choice is to attend Our Lord and Savior Church."

"Well, that's not my choice. Those white people are all stuck up. Besides, they treat us like poor, white ..."

"Hannah Barrington, don't you finish that sentence. People may treat us however they darn well please. It doesn't make it so, nor do we have to act like it is. Now, let's get going. We've got further to walk, and I'd prefer not being late our first time there."

"But Ma, I don't think I can walk that far," Hannah whined.

"Don't give me that. If I've told you once, I've told you a hundred times, don't you let anyone treat you like a cripple, and that includes yourself. Now, let's go!"

Sitting in the pew between Rose and Grandpa Herb was the hardest part of attending church for Amberlin, particularly since her eyes seemed to have a mind of their own. They constantly wandered to the side wall where the newest tombstone plaque hung:

IN LOVING MEMORY OF OUR LOST ANGEL,
EVELYN LEE GENTRY
BORN SEPTEMBER 24, 1925 ~ DIED APRIL 28, 1945

Amberlin still remembered the first time she saw the plaque. She thought, I never have to worry about forgetting my birthday, because even though she hadn't been able to read all the words, she recognized April 28, 1945 as her birthday. It took her several days to get up the nerve to ask her Grandpa about it.

They were sitting together in the Sanctuary. Papa Herb had just finished reading her Alice's Adventures in Wonderland, one of Amberlin's favorite books, and had closed the cover. The two of them sat there contemplating the story. Finally, after taking a deep breath, Amberlin cleared her throat and asked. "Papa Herb?"

When her hesitation lengthened out to a pregnant pause, Papa Herb, prompted her. "Yes dear. Do you have something you want to talk about?"

"Yes, but I...I don't know how to start."

"Why not start by sharing what's on your mind?" That seemed easy enough so, after a few more seconds, Amberlin spoke up.

Ben dipped his body in a mock bow. "Detective Stover at your service."

Amberlin knew Ben enjoyed being an important part of the group. Most of the time, it felt like to her that he had to force himself to fit in, even with Hannah and her who knew him better than just about anyone else in the community.

He walked over to the closest door. "Someone shine your light down here so I can find the right key." Hannah obliged. He inserted the key and turned it, then looked back at them.

"Ready?"

The two girls nodded, but neither of them moved.

"What if we get caught?" Hannah asked.

"No one's going to catch us," Ben replied. "Everyone is asleep. We'll be in, find out what we need to know, and be out of here without anyone being the wiser... except us."

He opened the door, then stepped aside. "Ladies first."

"What's this? Suddenly you're a knight in shining armor?" Amberlin said as she squared her shoulders before finally taking a step forward.

"Don't worry. I'm sure it won't last." Hannah giggled nervously as she followed behind her friend. The two girls turned on their flashlights as they walked down the hall.

"Keep those shining down on the floor in front of us, so if someone does happen to drive by they won't see anything." Ben closed the door behind them but left it unlocked. Good idea, thought Amberlin, figuring it was best just in case they needed to make a quick getaway.

"Let me lead the way. I know this church like the back of my hand. Hell, I've spent most of my life wandering around these old halls."

"Would you mind not swearing while we're in church?" Amberlin whispered. "I'd kinda like to keep God on our side if you know what I mean?"

"Whatever you say. You're the boss."

Hannah handed him her flashlight and waited for him to lead the way down the hall to the burial vaults.

There were about half-a-dozen vaults on this side of the church, each one with a small plaque giving the name of the person along with their birth date and the date they died. They found Evelyn Gentry's vault easily.

"Damn...I mean darn," Ben said as he shined his light on the plaque.

"What's wrong?" Amberlin asked.

"I forgot. Stupid of me. Of course, the vaults are locked as well."

"Well, don't you have the keys there?" Hannah asked.

"Not on this key ring," Ben replied. "But I know where they are. Stay here. I'll go get them. They're down in my father's desk drawer in his office."

"Maybe we should all go together," Hannah said with a waver in her voice. "I'm not sure we should split up."

"No, I can get there and back faster without you two," Ben replied already starting down the hall that led to Reverend Stover's office. "Hang loose. See how many books of the Bible you can remember. I'll be back before you get through the Old Testament."

"It'll be all right, Hannah," Amberlin said as she sat down near the door to her mother's vault and patted the floor next to her. "I appreciate you being here with me. You're right. This trip would have been too spooky without you."

"It's pretty spooky with me, if you ask me," Hannah replied as sat down next to Amberlin, throwing her braced leg out in front of her.

"Ssshhh," Ben hissed as his light faded down the hall. "You'll wake the dead."

His father's office was at the other end of the church, but it only took him a couple minutes to reach it. I sure hope those keys are still where they were the last time I saw them, he thought. What if someone had borrowed them and failed to return them? The mission would end before it hardly had begun. As he entered the office, he shined his light over to the desk and was careful to not bump into either of the chairs that set in front of it. He opened the top left drawer, and shined his light in it, then breathed a sigh of relief. The keys were right where they were supposed to be.

He picked them up and was almost to the office door when a sudden bright light stopped him in his tracks.

"Whatcha got there honey?"

Ben heart tried to leap out of his rib cage at the sound of his mother's voice.

"What the...what are you...? You scared the living bejesus out of me."

"Getting caught being somewhere you oughtn't to be will do that," Missy replied as she rose from the chair in the corner of the office.

"It took me a bit to figure out what in the world you three were up to, but then it came to me. That little no good Gentry girl is snooping around where she doesn't belong and dragging you and her other friend into it as well."

"She has a right to know what happened to her mother." Ben paused. How had his mother figured out what they were doing unless she knew something about Amberlin's mother herself? "What are we going to find in that vault, mother, and what do you know about all this?"

"That's none of your business. It's ancient history...history that's better left in the past, that is unless you want to ruin your father and me. You'll just have to take my word on that, but unless you want to end up in an orphanage or foster care, you'll do what you're told."

"So, you're not going to let us see what's in the vault, huh?"

Missy walked over to the desk and leaned against it. "Well, I've had some time to think and pray about it here in the dark, and here's the message I received."

"There's Ben's light coming down the hall now," Amberlin said. The two girls were both sitting on the floor with their backs against the wall, their sides touching each other. Amberlin gave Hannah's hand a last squeeze then stood up, and helped her friend rise as well.

"I sure hope he found the keys." Hannah brushed off the back of her jeans. "I sure don't want to have to come back and do this a second time."

"Me either." As Ben neared them, Amberlin whispered, "Did you find them?"

"You know, I'm not so sure we should be doing this. As it says on a lot of tombstones, 'rest in peace,'" Ben replied as he stopped a few feet from the door to the vault. "Maybe we should just chalk this up as one of my bad ideas."

Amberlin shined her flashlight on his face. It looked paler than normal. Was being in the church this late at night getting to him too?

"No, we're doing this," Amberlin replied. "At least I'm doing this. You two have done your part already, and I thank you for it. Now, if you have the key to the vault, Ben, I'll finish it from here."

Ben dug into his jean pocket and pulled out the key. "These old locks can be kind of tricky. You better let me do the honors."

He handed the flashlight back to Hannah so she could shine it on the vault door. He stuck the key in the lock. He pushed against the door with his shoulder while at the same time turning the key. He then pulled down on the latch and with a grating of metal on metal it opened.

Leaving the key in the lock, he pushed the door open and waved to the two girls. "Ladies first."

Amberlin took a deep breath as she stared into the black abyss in front of her. She felt Hannah's hand reaching for hers. Together they stepped into the vault, shining the lights in front of them.

The vault was smaller than Amberlin expected, probably no more than seven feet square she estimated. At the far end was a dark mahogany casket setting on a concrete shelf that projected from the far wall.

The silence and stillness felt like it could be cut with a knife. Slowly, Amberlin took a step towards her mother's coffin, then a second and third. Holding her light and Papa Herb's crowbar in one hand, and Hannah's hand in the other, she shined the light around the casket looking for the best way to open it.

That's when she heard the door close behind her close and a second later the key turn in the lock.

"What the..." Hannah said as the two of them turned to see what antics Ben was playing at this time, but there was no Ben—just the solid closed and locked door.

They were trapped.

The two girls stood in shocked silence for several seconds trying to get their heads around what had just happened. Finally, Amberlin rushed over to the door, and tried the latch just to confirm what she already knew — the door was locked.

She pounded on the door with the crowbar. "Alright, funny boy. That's quite enough kidding around. Open the door and let's get on with this." She waited several seconds, then when she didn't hear anything from the other side, she pounded on the door again, this time harder and longer.

"Ben! Ben! Open this door, do you hear me? Ben?"

She glanced back to Hannah, who was pressed against the coffin, looking like she was about to faint.

Amberlin walked back over to her friend. "I don't know what he thinks he's doing but I promise you, we'll be okay. I just know it."

Hannah nodded but when she opened her mouth, nothing came out but a small squeak.

Ben leaned against the other side of the door, his face twisted in pain. He could hear the clanks of the crowbar on the door better than he could hear Amberlin's voice. While it was difficult to make out the words clearly, he could hear and feel the anger mixed with fear coming from his friend. His heart ached to know he'd double-crossed the only two people in Golden Acres who really cared about him.

He started to turn around to unlock the door when Missy stepped from the shadows, a small pen light in her hand. "Uh uh, mustn't do that son. Just step away from the door. I'll take it from here." She pushed him away, then stepped to the door to remove the key.

"You go to the car and stay there. It's in your father's parking space. I'm just going to give them a good scare—one that will convince them to leave the past in the past."

He nodded, the ringing of Amberlin's voice still reverberating through his mind. "You are going to let them out, right?"

"Do what I said!" The steely tone of his mother's voice assured him there was no negotiating room. "I'll be out there in a little bit, and then we'll go home and fix some breakfast for your father and you."

Amberlin spent the next few minutes calming her friend, and in the process herself. She then walked around the vault checking every corner of it before returning to sit down beside Hannah.

"How, how does it look?" Hannah asked.

"Truth?"

"Yes."

"Best I can tell, the vault is air tight," Amberlin replied, watching her friend's face closely to see how she'd react to the news.

"Oh, that's not good, is it? What are we going to do?"

Amberlin could hear the panic starting to rise in Hannah's voice. "First thing, is we stay calm. The calmer we stay the less oxygen we'll use up and the more time we'll have to figure out how to get out of here."

Hannah nodded. "Okay, step one — stay calm. Then what?"

Amberlin paused for a moment before answering. "You know that special talent I seem to have to be able to sense what's going on inside another person?"

"Yeah, so? How's that going to help in this situation?"

"Well, it's not the only gift I have." Papa John had warned her never to share her special gifts with anyone, but this seemed to be the exception to that rule.

"Okay," Hannah said slowly. "So, can you maybe blow that door off its hinges or teleport us to the other side of it?"

Amberlin laughed. "Nothing quite so dramatic, but I may be able to unlock the door." She told Hannah about the time she'd changed the flow of the water spout in the tub several years ago.

"I've practiced on a few other things, like moving a pencil across a desk, relatively simple things."

"Sure. I mean anyone can move a pencil across a desk with their mind," Hannah said, then giggled, but Amberlin thought she heard an edge of hysteria in the laugh.

"I mean it's simple compared to trying to pick a lock, but let me give it a try."

They sat on the floor next to the door. "I think we better use just one light at a time. No telling how long the batteries will last."

Before she'd finished her sentence, Hannah had switched hers off. "Good idea. I would prefer not having to sit here in the dark if we can help it."

Amberlin closed her eyes as she tried to calm her own mind and to clear it of any unnecessary distraction. The two girls sat in silence for several minutes as Amberlin tried to move the small inner mechanism of the lock.

After several minutes, she opened her eyes looked at Hannah and shrugged. "Sorry. I was able to see the water in the tub and the pencil on the desk. If I could only see the insides of the lock that might help, but it's a lot harder moving something you can't see at all."

"Yes, I found that to be true myself," Hannah said, then laughed. Amberlin could hear the fear mounting in her friend this time.

She reached over and patted Hannah's knee. "Well, surely someone will come looking for us as soon as they figure out we're missing."

"Yes, I'm sure they will," Hannah replied. "I just don't know that they're going to know to look in your dead mothers vault."

"Good point." Amberlin felt her own calmness begin to crack.

The two girls sat in silence for several minutes. Finally, Amberlin stood up.

"What now?" Hannah asked. "Do you have another idea on how to get us out of here?"

"No, not yet, but I came here to find out about my mother, so I'm going to complete our mission no matter what."

She walked over to the coffin and again shined the light on it, looking for the best way to open the lid.

"How about helping me." She figured if nothing else, it might take Hannah's minds off their predicament for just a little while.

Hannah rose and turned on her light. "Maybe a little extra light will help, just for a few minutes."

Together the two girls started prying open the casket until finally the lid was ready to be removed. Amberlin looked at her friend. "Okay, it's time to find out if my mother is still alive or not."

She slowly raised the lid, and the two of them pointed their lights into the rectangle of darkness.

Missy slid into the driver's seat. She put the key in the ignition but didn't turn the car on. Instead, she sat there in the darkness and silence. Finally, she turned to her son.

"I told you earlier that the past needed to stay in the past, but there's a part of that past I think you should know about. You'll be able to understand better why I'm doing what I'm doing."

She paused, waiting for Ben to say something, but when he didn't, she continued.

"Several years ago when you were still a baby, your dad was visited by an evil force in the form of Evelyn Gentry."

"Amberlin's mother?"

"Yes, Evelyn was a disturbed young lady. Some called her wild, others called her a free spirit, but I knew what she really was. She was possessed by a demon from hell, and while possessed she took a fancy to your father. Some demons are sent here to try to unseat powerful men of God like your father. This one almost succeeded."

"What happened?" Ben asked.

Continuing to stare at her son to see what his reaction would be, she replied, "Evelyn seduced your father to have illicit sex with her, and Amberlin was the result."

Ben turned to look at her, a confused look of astonishment on her face. "My father is Amberlin's father? Why, that would make us..."

"Half brother and sister," Missy completed his sentence. "Yes, that's right. But I couldn't let the demon win. If the truth had gotten out, it would have ruined your father...it would have ruined us and all that we've built here.

"You see, son, it wasn't just Evelyn. It's the whole Gentry family. They're agents of Satan, and they must be stopped. The cancer of this community known as the Gentrys must be cut out if this community is to survive. I've simply been called by God to be the surgeon in this case."

"So what really happened to Evelyn?"

"That's none of yours or anyone else's business. Let's just say that the Lord stepped in and won over the devil once again, as he's about to do once more. Now, let's go home. I need to talk with your father."

"Why, it's empty," Hannah said as she looked up at her friend.

"No, not quite," Amberlin replied. "There's just no body in it, but there's something in it." She moved her light around. "There's just stuff... a bunch of someone's stuff."

She reached down and pulled out a framed picture. "It's the woman in my dream," she said looking at the photo. She set the picture down on the floor and pulled out another object—a hair brush, which she set on the floor next to the photo.

"And what's this, a sweater?" She held the garment up to the light of Hannah's flashlight. It was light pink and soft, probably cashmere, she thought. She held it to her chest and inhaled its fragrance. It smelled like a lilac bush in spring. As she took a second whiff, her mind suddenly flashed. She felt her eyes roll back in her head.

In her mind's eye, she saw the lady of the photograph except she was older this time. Once again, Amberlin felt a strong connection of love and intimacy, but this time it didn't feel like a memory from the past. It felt like the two of them were connected right here and now.

Could it be? If her mother was alive, was it not possible that they could be connected in some way through space and time? If so, maybe, just maybe her mother could help get them out of this fix. It was worth a try.

"Mother...dear sweet mother. Please help me. I'm your daughter, Amberlin. My friend and I are locked in a vault in the church in the center of Golden Acres Christian Community where you once lived. If you can hear me, please help. We're locked in here, and I don't know how much more air we have. Contact your father, my grandfather, Papa Herb. Help us! Help us please!"

Amberlin started to repeat the message but blacked out before she could finish it.

CHAPTER TWELVE
The Message

WE carry with us the wonders we seek outside us. Thomas Browne

IT WAS DURING THE EARLY morning hours before dawn, before the birds begin to welcome the new day, in the darkest part of night, when the tossing and turning of a fitful sleep may finally give way to a deep, relaxing, dream filled sleep, when Spooks received Amberlin's message. Because she was in the deep REM stage of sleep, the message came through loud and clear—so loud that it woke her, and for that reason she remembered the message into her waking state.

She reached under her bed and pulled out the pad of paper, the water colors and the brush she'd *borrowed* from the arts and craft room a few days before. She wrote down the essential part of the message before it disappeared like so many fragments of previous dreams.

She had no doubt the dream-induced message was real, and that it had come from her daughter. *My daughter,* she thought. *Oh God, I really do have a daughter, and she's in danger, trapped in a small room and running out of air.*

Spooks painted furiously, trying to capture every important detail, but even as she wrote, she wondered *how am I going to get this to someone who will believe me in time? The only person in the whole Asylum who might believe such a bizarre story might already be leaving for the day.*

She didn't know the exact time, but it felt like three or four o'clock in the morning, and Miriam shift ended at five. She had maybe an hour to alert Miriam, but she was locked in her room, with no one scheduled to come back until after Miriam would have already left.

She finished the message and reviewed her work:

x

Daughter - Golden Acres C. C.
Trapped Vault
Call Papa Herb - HELP!

It was the best she could do. No, wait. Papa Herb. That name rang a distinct bell in her memory. That's my father. A cloudy image floated into her mind. But what was his last name...my last name?

She closed her eyes and tried to relax her mind, to allow the answer that she knew must be someone in her bank of memories to float to the surface.

GENT

What was that? Did that mean he was a gentleman or was that his last name or at least part of it? She decided to include it in her message, crammed in between "Herb" and "Help."

Sure, the message was now clear as mud, but it was the best she could do, and time was running out. It didn't matter how clear or unclear the message was if she couldn't get it to Miriam before she left...but how?

Miriam might just show up before she ended her shift, but getting this message to her was far too important to count on a "might." Spooks walked over to the door and tested it to assure herself that it was, indeed, locked tight.

She got down on her hands and knees and felt along between the bottom of the door and the floor where she found a good half to three-quarter inch gap. That should be plenty of room to slide the note through, but then what?

The answer came like a flashbulb igniting within her mind. Just one thing to do. She checked to be sure the paint was dry, and then pushed the piece of paper under the door. Good. That was the simple part. This next part would take a lot more concentration, but her daughter's life was at stake. That was plenty of motivation to keep her focused on the task at hand.

The paper laid on the floor of the hallway for several seconds, still and undisturbed...until suddenly it fluttered like a mild summer breeze catching under it. It rose an inch or two then settled back to the floor.

On the other side of the door, Spooks sat with her back against the door and visualized the paper blowing down the hallway in the direction of the nurses' station...and the paper slowly obliged, moving inch by slow inch, as though pulled by some invisible string—the invisible string of Spooks' will.

"Where's Ben? Is he still sleeping?" Rev. Stover asked as he sat down for breakfast.

"I'm famished. I could eat..."

"Ben has been restricted to his room. I need you to sit down, be quiet, and listen," Missy said as she sat down next to him and poured them both a cup of coffee.

"I...am...sitting," he replied in a disgruntled voice. "What's going on here? Why is Ben restricted..."

"Listen!" Missy yelled, then took a deep breath, trying to calm her nerves. "I need you just to listen to me now. Ben did something really stupid last night. He's forced my hand, and now I just have to...we just have to follow through and not lose our nerve. God's will prevails," she said as she crossed herself.

"Sweetie, we're not Catholic."

"I know that, you...!" She breathed again. "I just figure it can't hurt right now."

"What in the world is going on?"

"I don't have time to go into the details. Besides, the fewer details you know, the better. The bottom line is that Amberlin knows her mother is alive, and it's just a matter of time before she finds out who her real father is."

"How in the world...?" but the glare from his wife stopped the question in mid-sentence.

"I need you to call an emergency meeting of the Community Council, making sure everyone is there except Rose. I want you to show them these pictures." She pulled the photos she'd taken at the Gentrys from the pocket of her apron.

"Inform the council that you've been concerned for some time that the Gentry family had fallen from God's grace, that they've been worshipping idols and giving in to the temptation of Satan.

"You must convince them that this family is evil and have been possessed by the demons of Hell. I know you can do this. Just bring all the powers of your Sunday fire and brimstone sermons and don't let anyone leave that meeting until they are one-hundred percent convinced that Rose and Herb Gentry are the devils incarnate."

"Missy, my dear. Rose has been your best friends for years. Why would you want to spread such a story about her?"

"She's never been my friend," Missy answered with a look of disdain. "I've fooled you just like I've fooled everyone else into believing this because it served my purpose. She's been the bane of my life. It's always been Rose this, and Rose that. Rose is so smart, so well organized, so able, such a wonderful Christian. When all along it's simply been because she happened to have been born a Gentry.

"Well, no more. Today is the day of reckoning; the day the wrath of God brings down the Gentry dynasty."

Missy stood up and started towards the door, then paused and turned back to her husband. "Have the meeting at the Waldens."

"Why there?" Rev. Stover asked.

"Two reasons—they are staunch supporters of what we're building here. Also, it's much less likely Rose will get wind of the meeting if you meet somewhere other than here or at the church.

"Also, remember, it was your weakness and sinful ways that started all this. I'm just doing what needs to be done so we can continue God's work here. Don't you dare let either one of us down."

CHAPTER THIRTEEN
Stover's Confession

WE are made wise not by the recollection of our past, but by the responsibility for our future. George Bernard Shaw

***

GOLDEN ACRES 1945

Missy had put up with Rev. Stover acting strange for well over a week. She realized he was prone to getting into moods from time to time, but they seldom lasted for more than a day or two. Whatever it was bugging him, it was now getting on her nerves so tonight she planned to find out what it was.

They were lying in bed, both reading from their Bibles as they did every night before retiring. It was also a time when she could often catch her husband with his guard down. In short, it was the perfect time to find out what he'd been withholding from her.

Missy closed her Bible with a little slap and patted it lightly where it lay on her ample bosom. She paused a moment, considering whether to use the slow, southern charm approach or the more direct, get-to-the-point method. Considering the hour and how tired she was, besides the fact that she'd already spent the day as she did every day being southern nice, she decided to cut to the chase.

"Okay, Benjamin, tell me what's troubling you."

"Why my dear, I have no idea what you're talking about. Everything is just fine," Rev. Stover replied as he slowly closed his Bible and placed it on the table beside him.

"Okay, if that's the story you want to stick to, I can wait you out. Of course, that means very little if any sleep tonight because I know something is troubling you, and I don't plan to go to sleep tonight until you tell me what it is."

She twisted in bed so she could look directly at his profile. "Ben, you've been moody and out of sorts for at least a week, and that's simply not like you. Something is up, and if I know you, it's something you feel you've done wrong. You're so hard on yourself. But you know what they say, 'confession is good for the soul,' so come along now. Confess to me what's going on."

The room was quiet for a moment, and the first warning Missy had that she'd hit a soft spot was a stifled sob from her husband of close to five years. She often told people that he had been worth waiting for, though the truth be told, she had just about decided she'd end up an old maid after still being single in her mid-thirties. So, when the new minister showed up, she'd wasted no time sinking her claws into him. Missy could be mighty persuasive when she set her mind to it.

She glanced over to his side of the bed and was shocked to see two streams of tears making their way to his well-defined chin. "Why, what in the world? What is it Benjamin?" She asked, afraid for the first time that it might be something serious.

"Oh, Missy, I have sinned mightily in the eyes of God. I'm a weak and sinful man," he wailed, wiping the tears with the back of his hand.

Missy didn't quite know what to make of these antics, so she figured it best to be silent and to see what emerged. It didn't take long.

"You know that young woman, Evelyn Gentry, that goes to our church?"

"Of course I do, silly man. She's Rose's daughter, and least you forget Rose has been my best friend for over twenty-five years."

"Yes, yes, of course. How could I forget? You and Rose do go way back to your childhood years. It's nice to have such friends..."

"What about Evelyn?" Missy said with a little edge to her voice.

After a long pause, Ben finally whispered, "She's been coming to me for the past several weeks for counseling. She's a troubled girl. Much more troubled than anyone knows. She hides it well."

"Okay...I'm sorry to hear that. Is that it?"

"No, not quite. Well, over the past few weeks, as I've helped her to take her troubles to Jesus, she's grown...well attached. You know how that can happen."

Missy felt the hackles on the back of her neck stand up. Not a good sign. "You're not telling me everything, are you? What aren't you telling me? Spit it out."

Rev. Stover took a deep breath. "Evelyn seduced me."

"She what!" Missy flew out of bed. "What did you just say?"

"Now, now, calm down. You'll wake little Ben."

"I'll do more than wake him. I'll bundle him up and take him right out of here if you don't answer my question and tell me the truth. None of your lying to protect your sweet ass."

"Now, darling, please watch your language. We just finished..."

"Don't give me any of your pious crap to deflect this conversation from the real dirt. I know Evelyn and I know you. If I had to guess who did the seducing, I'd put my money on you and your one-eyed grass snake that you can't seem to keep in your pants."

Rev. Stover sighed. "It gets worse, I'm afraid."

Missy groaned. "Go on."

"Evelyn is pregnant with my child, and she won't consider an abortion, and she's threatened to tell Rose all about the affair."

"Oh my God, Ben. Evelyn is only seventeen. What have you done?" It was now Missy's turn to wipe the tears from her eyes.

"Well, we men have needs. You know that and well, with little Ben coming along, and you're not in the mood.... I'm sorry, honey. I truly am. I'm a weak, sinful man; I am."

"You can say that again." Missy took a couple of deep breaths, trying to calm herself. "If this gets out, it will ruin us and everything that we're building here in Golden Acres. You're the pastor of hundreds of good Christian folk. How could you be so thoughtless? How could you do this to me?"

Rev. Stover sat on the side of the bed his elbows on his knees as he ran his fingers through his thick, black hair that was just beginning to show a hint of gray. "I know...I know. I'm so sorry. Can you ever forgive me?"

A part of Missy's brain woke up with that question. It was a pretty good question. Would she be able to forgive him, or was this the end of the marriage. She played out the various scenarios. Here she was with a new child less than a year old, no college education and no real skills beyond being a good homemaker and a minister's wife. Where would she go if she couldn't forgive him and ended up leaving him?

She'd probably end up working a double shift at Woolworth's or some waitressing job just to make ends meet. Or she'd have to move home with her mother. No, no way would she put herself or her son under that woman's thumb again.

Finally, she looked over at her husband, the answer to his question crystal clear in her mind.

"Yes, I will forgive you..." She paused to make sure the rest of the sentence had the impact she intended. "But I'll never forget what you did, and I don't want you to forget what I'm going to have to do to get us through this mess. Do you understand me, Ben Stover? And if you ever...ever so much as look at another woman, I'll separate you from your one-eyed pet that has gotten you into all this trouble. And that's a promise!"

Since neither of them had slept well the night before, it wasn't until the third cup of coffee that Rev. Stover had the nerve to speak up. He started with the question that had been on his mind most of the night.

"So, what's your plan?"

"Who says I have a plan? It's your problem, isn't it? I don't recall sleeping with anyone other than my husband. How about you?"

Rev. Stover sighed. "I probably deserved that."

"Oh, my dear sweet husband, you deserve that and so much more."

"I seem to remember you mentioned that you planned to do something to get us through this mess. Besides, you always have a plan. That's one of the things I love about you."

"Don't you dare talk to me about love...not now. Not until I tell you it's okay to use that word around me." Missy slammed a plate of eggs, bacon and toast in front of him. "And yes, you're right. God did come to me during the night with a plan. I guess he's quicker to forgive you than I am."

He shoveled a fork full of eggs into his mouth. "So, wha..yu..plamm?"

"Well, you said it yourself last night. Evelyn is a much more troubled girl than anyone knows. Well, our job is to let them know. It's the Christian thing to do...you know, so she can get the love and support she needs from her Christian community."

"But you know that what is shared in counseling sessions are strictly confidential. I shouldn't have even told you what I did last night."

"Oh, poppycock. You leave everything to me. Gossip is a very powerful instrument in the right hands, and I know how to weld it most effectively." She placed her own plate on the table, then went back to the stove for the coffee pot. "What's the name of that drifter that's been hanging around the past few weeks?"

"You mean Handyman Harry? That's all I've heard people call him. Why?"

"I've noticed he's been paying a lot of attention to Evelyn, that's why." She topped off their two cups of coffee and plopped down in the chair across from him.

"He's been doing a fair amount of work on the Gentry's home if that's what you mean."

"Exactly. By the time I'm through, it'll be no question in anyone's mind that he's the father of that little bastard baby. You only need to do two things for this to all work out okay."

"What's that?"

"First, you need to convince Evelyn that it's in everyone's best interest to not say who the daddy is."

"How am I supposed to do that?"

"I don't know. That's for you to figure out. Bribe her, threaten her, blackmail her if you have to. Just be sure she keeps her trap shut...at least until the rumor mill has had a chance to get in gear. After that, it'll be her word against yours, and half the other members of the community."

"And what's the second thing?"

"Keep your pet snake in your pants."

One thing Missy knew about herself was that she was a great gardener, though not in the classical sense. Dirt was...well, just too dirty. No, her gardening talents laid in planting seeds and watching them grow in the gossip garden of the community.

Truth be told, that was how she, a plain girl with a plain personality was able to hook the number one catch of the season several years ago when a young, dynamic minister took the job as associate pastor. Yes, Missy was good at managing the gossip garden, so it produced a bumper crop of exactly what she wanted from life. That is, what God and she wanted for her life.

Planting seeds about the handyman drifter and what he might really be up to at the Gentrys was fairly easy. After all, the women of Golden Acres seldom had such juicy gossip to talk about, so her seeds flourished in the rich soil with only a little watering from Missy.

By the time Evelyn started showing her baby bump, everyone naturally assumed the drifter to be the daddy. Everyone but Evelyn herself.

"She told me she didn't care who people thought the daddy was," Rev. Stover said as he poured himself a second glass of scotch and dropped in a couple ice cubes. "She doesn't plan to say anything, but well, I don't know that we can trust her. I mean, what happens if two or three years from now, she decides to name me as the father. Even worse, what if the child is a boy and it looks just like me?"

Missy sat back and played with the ice in her almost empty glass. She'd still not completely forgiven him for what he'd done, but the sting had diminished over time, especially with the royal treatment she'd received from him since his confession.

"You make some good points there, for sure. There are two issues here. How to make sure Evelyn doesn't name you as the father in the short term, and how to keep her trap shut over the long haul as well. Let's bring this to God in prayer, Reverend. I know we can trust him to guide us through these trials and tribulations."

She placed her drink on the coaster, knelt down in front of the sofa and pulled her husband down beside her. They prayed for several minutes in silence; then Missy finished with "in Jesus name we pray. Thank you, God."

Rev. Stover stood up and brushed off his pants, then looked at Missy.

"Well, did you get anything?"

"Silly question from a silly boy. Of course, God always answers my prayers."

"So, what are we to do."

"You are simply to continue treating me like royalty while I go pay a visit to our good friends, the Gentrys."

Later that evening, it took Missy longer than usual to coax a colicky baby Ben to sleep, finally resorting to giving him a teaspoon of Paregoric before retiring to her bedroom. It had been an exhausting yet satisfying day. She'd just received word from her good friend that Herb Gentry had accepted the magazine assignment that would take him out of the country for close to a month — one more important step falling into place.

She finished washing her face and brushing her teeth, then walked into the bedroom where her husband lay reading his Bible.

"Well, it's all coming together," she said as she pulled the covers back on her side and climbed in beside him.

"What's coming together?" Rev. Stover asked as he closed his Bible, keeping his place with a finger.

It was just the response Missy wanted. "Remember several months ago when this fiasco of yours started, I told you to remember what it was going to take for me to get us through this mess?"

"Yes, dear, I remember, and you've done an amazingly thorough job. Evelyn has kept her mouth shut, and it seems like everyone just assumes Handyman Harry was the father, just as you said they would."

"Yes, it's gone well so far," Missy continued. "Now the next phase is about to start, and it's far more challenging."

"And what's that?"

"Making sure this problem goes away for...ever."

"And how do you plan on doing that?" Rev. Stover turned towards her, a concerned look on his face.

"Never you mind. The less you know about it, the better. That way, if something doesn't go right, you can honestly say you didn't have a clue about it."

"Missy, this sounds serious. What are you planning?"

"I'm planning to make sure that God's work continues here in Golden Acres, and no one, especially no one with the last name of Gentry, will get in my way...I mean in God's way. Now, turn out the light and let's get some sleep. Tomorrow is another big day."

CHAPTER FOURTEEN
Special Delivery

THERE are two kinds of talent, man-made talent and God given talent. With man-made talent you have to work very hard. With God given talent, you just touch up once in a while. Pearl Bailey

THE ASYLUM 1957

Miriam placed the last few records back in the filing cabinet and looked around the nurse's station to make sure everything was neat and orderly...just as Nurse Rankin insisted it be kept.

Satisfied by what she saw, she pulled her sweater from the back of the chair and draped it over her shoulders. One more day without any major mishap was one more successful day at her work, she thought, then wondered, Is this how it starts? Is this how the apathy and lack of compassion and care slowly seep in and takes over?

She sighed, too tired to be concerned with it now. It was almost 5 am and her shift was about to end. She'd think about it tomorrow. She thought about checking in on the patients one last time, but then remembered she'd promised to take her mother shopping today. She needed to get home and get at least a few hours of sleep.

The paper inched its way down the hall. Spooks could only move it only about six inches before she had to rest her mind. Even so, she was developing one royal migraine headache. It was causing her to see a sparkling haze around the objects in her room as well as heightening her sense of smell to super sensitive level.

Each time she thought of stopping to try to relieve her pain she remembered the image of the young girl she'd seen less than an hour before in her mind's eye. She looks so much like I did at that age, she thought. No way could she stop. Her daughter's life depended on it.

She was about to start again when she heard a sound of someone coming down the hall. Could it be Miriam? She pushed herself up from the floor, slowly standing to look through the window as Jeremy, the attendant on duty that night, passed by. She felt him stop several yards down the hall. She focused her mind back on the paper just as Jeremy bent down, picked up the paper, glanced at it, then balled it up and jammed it in his pocket.

"Noooo! Jeremy, you idiot. Come back here. Leave the paper where it was." She slowly collapsed against the door. "Pleassee! Come back.... Please...please God help me."

Miriam turned out the light in the nurses' station, picked up her pocketbook and started towards the exit, her mind already on her family and the many obligations waiting for her at home.

As she walked down the hall, she passed Jeremy coming up the hall from the patients' rooms. She nodded at him.

"Everything quiet down there?"

"Quiet as a church cemetery at midnight."

"Well, good night then. I'll see you tomorrow."

"You have a pleasant time with your family. Miss Miriam. You sure do deserve it."

She had her hand on the exit door when she heard Jeremy call her name. She turned back. Now, what? Please let it be nothing. I need my rest.

"Miss Miriam. I picked this up in the hall. Don't reckon it's anything but trash but thought..." He handed her the balled up piece of paper.

"What's this? Why is it balled up, Jeremy? She said as she began to straighten it out.

"Like I said, I figured it was just trash."

"Then why are you handing it to me?"

"I dunno. Just suddenly felt like the thing to do."

She flattened the paper out and looked at the message painted on it.

"Oh Lord, it's going to be a long day."

Miriam turned back to the nurses' station where she redeposited her purse and sweater. She rushed down the hall towards Spook's room to find out what the message meant, but as she approached Spook's door she ran into Nurse Rankin coming in for her shift.

"Why, what are you still doing here?"

Good morning to you, too, Miriam thought but decided, under the circumstances, it was best to stay on Nurse Rankin's good side...if she had one.

"I still need to check on something with one of the patients, and then I'll be on my way."

"Which patient?" Nurse Rankin asked, a tone of suspicion already building in her voice.

"Ahh, well, Spooks. I'll just be a minute. You go on to work, and I'll be down in just a few minutes."

"Nurse Miriam. You were officially off the clock, ten minutes ago. Tell me what you need from Spooks, and I'll check in with her sometime during my shift."

Miriam could see Spooks' face through the window of her door, trying to mouth something to her without drawing Nurse Rankin's attention, but she couldn't make out what it was.

"Ahhhhh, you're right. It's not that important. I'll check in with her in the next day or so." She turned to walk back to the nurses' station, hoping Nurse Rankin wouldn't follow, but, of course, she did.

How was she going to follow up on Spook's message with Nurse Rankin hovering over her? The answer was clear—she wasn't. She'd just have to work it out herself. She couldn't afford to lose her job and at the same time, she'd promised Spooks she would help, and she aimed to keep that promise.

The two women walked down the hall without speaking. When they arrived at the nurses' station, Miriam picked up her purse and sweater and turned to leave.

"I'll see you later," she said as light and breezy as she could muster.

Nurse Rankin nodded without saying anything. She was already looking over the charts for the day and had evidently already dismissed her colleague.

Do I dare sneak down to Spook's room now? But even as she asked herself the question, she noticed Rankin glance up at her. Like a hawk — a hawk watching her next meal. So, instead of turning towards the wards, she turned toward the door leading to the parking lot.

Her journey took her by Dr. Allen's office. As she walked by, she paused for a moment and glanced through the door's window. Dr. Allen wasn't in yet. He often arrived late to work, sometimes not coming in until eight or even nine o'clock. Miriam tried turning the doorknob and found it unlocked.

She quietly opened the door and slipped into his office. She kept the lights off to minimize the chance of drawing anyone's attention. As she approached Dr. Allen's desk, she pulled the note from her pocket and studied it again:

Daughter - Golden Acres C C

Trapped Vault

Call Papa Herb GENT - HELP!

This shouldn't be so difficult, she thought, now that I've had a few minutes to digest this.

Daughter, of course, must mean Spooks' daughter; the baby who she's been dreaming about, but wait a minute. She wouldn't be a baby now. Spooks had been a patient at the Asylum for over a decade, so her daughter would be a young girl by now.

Golden Acres C C what could that mean? The answer popped to her mind. She remembered visiting such a place once with her mom when she was a young girl herself. They toyed with the idea of moving there, but the visit convinced them it wasn't the kind of Christian community either one of them wanted to live in. Was that where Spooks was from? Had someone at Golden Acres had her committed here? It was all starting to make sense.

Trapped Vault? Now, that didn't make much sense, except that if Spook's daughter was in some trouble as the note and the HELP! clearly said, then she might be trapped in some kind of vault.

She looked down at the last line: Call Papa HerbGENT

Was he the one who'd had Spooks committed? No, probably not. If so, he'd probably be the last person Spooks would want me to call. No, he must be someone Spooks feels she can trust to help her daughter. It looked like Spooks had jammed in the word, "GENT", after the rest had been written. Did that mean that he was a gentleman, someone that could be trusted? Or could it be his name, meaning it was also Spooks' last name. Had she started to remember those important details?

Miriam picked up the phone and waited for the operator to answer. "Yes, operator, I need the phone number for someone who may live in the Golden Acres Christian Community. I think that's near Hallow Rock, but I'm not sure. The person's name is Herb Gent, or it might be listed as Herbert."

She waited as the operator looked up the number, her fingers strumming on the desk.

"I don't have a listing for a Herb or Herbert Gent?"

"Are you sure? This is very important. Someone's life could be at stake. Do you have any listing similar in the area?"

After another excruciating pause during which Miriam felt sure someone would catch her in Dr. Allen's office, the operator came back on the line.

"There's a Herbert S. Gentry in the Hallow Rock area."

"That must be it," Miriam said as she barely kept herself from dancing a jig right there in her boss's office.

"That number if 686-455-4450."

"Thank you, Operator. You're a dear."

Miriam clicked the button down on the phone to break the connection, and then when she heard a dial tone again, she dialed the number. As she did so, she prayed, Please be home, and please, Dear God, have this be the right Herb Gentry.

Miriam waited for the phone to begin ringing as she nervously tapped her nails on the desk, keeping her eyes on the office door while praying feverishly that no one would enter and that someone...the right someone would pick up the other end of the line.

Finally, after what seemed like an interminable length of time, the connection was made, and the phone began to ring...and ring...and ring.

"Pick up, please pick up...pick up the..."

"Hello," a man's voice came on the line. Miriam glanced from the door to the ceiling and mouthed, thank you God, before saying, "Hello, this is Nurse Miriam Mason calling for Mr. Herb Gentry," then held her breath.

"Yes, this is he. How may I help you?"

Suddenly, Miriam realized she didn't know what to say next. Who was this man, and what was his relationship to Spooks? Oh God, she didn't even know Spooks real name. It had been an issue for her from the very beginning, that all the pertinent information about the patients had been blacked out on all the records. They had all been turned into case number and nicknames only.

"Mr. Gentry, please be patient while I try to explain the purpose of my call. I work at a hospital for the mentally ill not too far from where you live. I received a rather strange and incomplete message from one of our patients this morning that included your name."

"Yes?" She could hear in that one word a world of concern already growing in Gentry's mind. She decided the best approach was to yank the bandage off quickly and pray it would all work out.

"Mr. Gentry, do you have a granddaughter, and if so, do you know where she is at this very moment?"

There was a long pause on the other end. "What is this all about, Miss...did you say your name was Mason?"

"Yes, Miriam Mason. Please call me Miriam." She tried to sound as kind and compassionate as possible, realizing her question could also be the type of question a kidnapper might ask to bring terror into a parent's heart to get them to comply with the ransom demands.

"Well then, call me Herb...while you explain just exactly what this is all about."

"As I said, I received a strange message from one of our patients. It was cryptic and incomplete, but it included your name, the name of the community you live in you do live in Golden Acres Christian Community?"

"Yes, that's right." The sound of his voice grew warmer now, less suspicious.

"I know this must come as a shock to you, but it's possible that your granddaughter is in grave danger. I hope that I'm wrong. That's why I asked if you know where she is right now."

"Why, she's upstairs in her bedroom asleep. It's only... 5:30 in the morning."

"Are you absolutely sure she's still there? Would you please do me a great favor and check?" Miriam heard and felt the tone of desperation in her voice. "If she's there, I'll owe you a huge apology and I promise I'll hang up and never disturb you again."

She heard a heavy sigh on the other end, but also motion. "Okay, Nurse Mason, but if this is a joke, it's a sick one and you belong in the hospital you purport to work at. I'll be back in a minute. Amberlin's room is just down the hall."

As Miriam waited, she prayed that the young girl named Amberlin was, indeed, still in her bed and that she'd owe Herb Gentry a huge apology. Of course, if that were the case, there'd still be the mystery of Spooks' message to solve.

Even before Herb returned to the line, she had her answer, and it threatened to rip her heart out, as she heard him shout, "Rose, Rose, wake up...wake up. Something has happened to Amberlin. She's not in her room."

"Hello...are you still there?" an out of breath Herb asked.

"Yes, I'm still here."

"Amberlin is not in her room. Oh my God, my dear girl...do you know where she is, and what's going on here?"

Miriam read the note to him word for word, then paused as he repeated it, probably so Rose could hear it.

"And where did you say you got this note from?"

"One of our patients. I'm sorry, but I'm not at liberty to say from whom specifically." It felt easy to use that legitimate reason rather than try to explain that she didn't know her patients' real names.

"Read it to me again...please." Miriam read it again.

"The missing piece here is "trapped vault," Herb said after a moment of silence. Obviously whoever this Herb Gentry was, he still had a sharp mind that he used well under pressure. "We've pretty much established that the daughter is probably my granddaughter...wait a minute. The note is about my granddaughter, but the way it's written would imply that it came from my daughter, Evelyn, but Miss Mason, my daughter has been dead for over ten years."

Before Miriam could reply, she heard a commotion in the background on the line and Herb talking to someone else.

"I'm afraid I'll have to call you back in a minute. My wife says she can shed some light on this. What's your number there?"

Oh no, I can't stay here. What if Dr. Allen walks in before he calls back? "Herb, I can't stay on this line any longer, but I'm only a few minutes from home. Give me ten minutes to get there and call me at this number...."

It had been hours since the vault door slammed shut, leaving Amberlin and Hannah locked in with what turned out to be an empty casket. Well, not completely empty, but thankfully without a body. Instead, Amberlin found it partially filled with items that clearly belonged to her mother.

Hannah's flashlight had died some time ago, and so they were left with only Amberlin's light. They decided to turn it on every few minutes then turn it off again and count to a hundred slowly before turning it back on.

Amberlin noticed when it was Hannah's turn to count, she counted faster and faster to keep the time in the dark as short as possible, but she decided not to say anything about it. After all, it was her fault her friend was in this mess in the first place. She tried several times to apologize to Hannah for getting her in such trouble, but each time she tried, her friend stopped her.

"No one twisted my arm or forced me to do this," Hannah said with a forced smile that made Amberlin want to cry. "I've never had a friend like you. You've been so good to me, never treating me as though I was less than..."

"That's because you're not. You're an incredible person. I thank God for the day you walked into that Sunday school class."

"Yeah, stumbled in would be more like it...and late to boot."

"Posh. However you came; I'm sure glad you did."

"Yeah, it would be pretty lonesome sitting here by yourself."

"That's for sure."

Amberlin switched off the light and started counting to herself, whispering every time she passed a number ending in zero. They had to conserve their air, which seemed to be getting stuffier and harder to breath by the minute.

When the she turned the light back on, Hannah was staring at her, her face inches from hers.

"What if no one comes?"

"Someone will come. I just know it."

"But how could anyone come. No one knows we're here."

"That's not true. My mother knows."

"What are you talking about? We don't even know if your mother is alive...not really. We just know her body wasn't buried here like everyone made you believe."

Amberlin paused before replying, trying to make sure the edge of anger she felt from her friend's remarks didn't carry into her voice. "I know. Hannah, you've got to believe me. I know she's alive, and I believe with all my heart that she knows we're in trouble. We've just got to have faith."

But as the time slowly passed, and breathing became more labored, even Amberlin began to wonder if it had all just been a hallucination.

The next time she turned on the light, Hannah laid beside her, still breathing...barely, but without responding to Amberlin's attempts to wake her. Amberlin knew she'd not be far behind.

CHAPTER FIFTEEN
The Delivery

YOUR profession is not what brings home your paycheck. Your profession is what you were put on earth to do. With such passion and such intensity that it becomes spiritual in calling. Vincent Van Gogh

GOLDEN ACRES 1945

"It's so good of y' all to have me over for tea like this." Missy patted Rose's knee as she gazed around the Gentry's sunroom where Rose had set out tea. "It's been just too long since we've gotten together."

Rose smiled back at her friend. "Well, to be completely honest, I think it was you who asked to come visit...but never mind that, it has been too long. It's good to see you again, Missy. I mean, I know we see each other at church and in those endless committee meetings, but, well, we just never seem to find time just to chat."

"What did you want to talk to us about?" Evelyn asked in a far less convivial voice.

"My, if that isn't our direct speaking Evelyn," said Missy with a polite smile. "You haven't changed a bit...well, other than the obvious...and well, that's what I came to talk about. I want to make sure your baby gets the very best of care. All children are blessed souls in the eyes of our Father, so I wanted to assure you that, when your time comes, I'll be there for the three of you.

"As your mother knows quite well, I'm a fully trained midwife. It's something I feel is part of my calling...to help little souls to come into this life with as much love and compassion as possible."

"Why, that's very nice of you to offer, but I haven't yet decided whether to have the child at home or in the hospital," Evelyn replied.

Missy looked at Rose, a worried, almost frantic look on her face. "Why Rose, you must convince your daughter to stay away from those hospitals. They're the worst place in the world to have a baby. Why, hospitals are filled with sick and dying people. That's no place for a baby."

"Well, to be quite honest, Evelyn and I haven't had a chance to discuss this yet. This all came on us rather suddenly you understand."

"Why sure I do, and I don't mean to upset you or anything. As I said, I just want to be sure the little tike gets the very best care possible coming into this world and later as well. By the way, what do you think it is a boy or a girl?"

Evelyn smiled for the first time. "Oh, it's a girl. I'm sure of it."

"Well, whichever it is, I want to assure you that when the time comes, her or his education will be well taken care of. As you know, Reverend Stover and I helped start the scholarship fund a few years ago, and I'm the chairperson for the selection committee."

Missy looked from side to side, then leaned forward as though she was about to share the most important secret in the world. "You can rest assured the child's education will be well taken care of if you know what I mean."

"Well, we certainly don't expect any preferential treatment," Rose replied, "but we do appreciate the sincerity with which you mean it."

"Of course, we will have to tread lightly when the time comes. Wouldn't want anything to reflect badly on our Christian community here, now would we?" She glared long and hard at Evelyn to be sure the mother-to-be understood her meaning. "Discretion will need to be our watchword."

The two Gentry ladies sat in the parlor long after Missy had left. They sipped their tea and munched on the sandwiches that Rose had fixed for the occasion.

"Mama Rose, can I ask you a question?"

"Sure, child. What is it?"

"I'm not sure how to ask it."

"Well, asking it straight out might be refreshing given the conversation we just had."

Evelyn laughed. "For the life of me, I don't understand what you see in that woman."

"Now, now. Missy and I go way back. You know that. She's a good Christian woman. She's done a lot for this community."

"If you say so." Evelyn placed her teacup in its saucer and reached for the last wedge of sandwich. "Eating for two now, for sure. Here's my question, plain and simple. What do you think the chances are that my child will have the...uh, you know...the special something that makes you and me different from others."

Rose blanched at the mention of the powers that had plagued her since she was a young girl. "Oh my Lord, child, how do I answer that?" She paused. "All we can do at this point is to pray that she's not cursed as you and I have been."

Evelyn shook her head. She oughtn't to be surprised by her mother's response. It had been an issue between them for years, so much so that they'd finally mutually decided it was simpler to say as little about it as possible. But Evelyn didn't have anyone she could talk to about it — no one who'd had the actual experiences that she'd, and her mother shared.

She decided to try once more. "Oh, mama, I wished you didn't feel that way. I truly feel these powers are special gifts from God. I mean, after all, his son had some pretty special talents in his day, and didn't he tell his disciples we could have similar abilities and more?"

"Now, don't you go quoting scripture at me. I know from personal experiences that having such 'gifts,' as you call them, has been nothing but a royal pain in my life. I'm thankful that God finally intervened and took them away, and I pray every night he'll do the same for you...and now, I'll add your daughter to the prayer."

Well, I guess our prayers are just going to confuse God then, Evelyn thought but decided it best not to say. She'd just keep praying like she did most nights for God to help her use her gifts to do good in the world.

She decided it was best to change the subject. They'd already covered this ground so many times, there was no point in discussing it further. It would only lead to an argument, and that wouldn't be good for the baby, or for her for that matter.

"Do you think it's a girl, too?"

Rose smiled, obviously pleased to drop the subject as well. "Oh yeah, no question in my mind."

About two weeks before Evelyn's child was due, the drifter suddenly disappeared. No one ever suspected that Missy had paid him to leave, making him promise never to return to Golden Acres.

As the due date drew nearer, the excitement in the community was palpable. No one discussed, at least in public, about who the father might be. After all, they were southern ladies with a long tradition of being 'southern nice.' Besides, by this time everyone knew the drifter was the daddy, and since he was no longer in the picture, it was simply old news.

Over the course of the last few months, Rose had convinced Evelyn to allow Missy to be the midwife. After all, everyone recognized her to be the most experienced midwife in the surrounding six counties, and the other three midwives in the area were considered only borderline Christians. While that didn't really bother Evelyn, in an effort to keep the peace with Rose, she consented.

Papa Herb spent most of his spare time, when he wasn't working on a writing assignment, converting the spare bedroom next to Evelyn's room into the nursery. He suggested using a neutral color like a pale yellow just in case the child turned out to be a boy instead, but neither of the Gentry women would hear of it.

"I want the wallpaper to be pink, with white trim. I want laced curtains and a warm rug on the floor," Evelyn instructed him, and he was only too happy to oblige.

"I'm just saying if this child comes into the world and he's a boy, you're likely to scar him for life with all the pinkness, but it's your call."

Just days before Evelyn's due date, he received notice of a large assignment from one of the most prestigious magazines in the country offering more money than he'd ever received for an assignment with promises of more to come if he did a good job. Unfortunately, the research for the assignment would require him to travel overseas.

"You've got to take it," Evelyn said when he shared it with the family at dinner one night. "What good are you going to be here during the delivery, anyway? I'll be fine, and so will the baby. You just go do an excellent job and hurry home to meet your granddaughter."

"Well, that's what Rose said too. Doesn't feel quite right, but if you think I should take it as well, I will, but I won't leave until the nursery is finished. That's something I am good for."

"Oh, you're good for a lot of things, Papa," Evelyn said, as she reached out and grasped his hand. "Birthing babies just doesn't happen to be one of them."

Three days after Herb left on his writing assignment, Evelyn started having contractions. They started around 10:30 that night as Evelyn was preparing for bed. At first she hoped it was simply indigestion but when the third, then fourth one came in short order, she knew a long night was ahead.

As she walked down the hall towards her mother's bedroom, she felt another contraction, followed a few seconds later with a rush of fluids.

"Oh, brother," she gasped leaning against the wall for support. When the pain subsided, she resumed walking, this time with more urgency.

"Mama Rose, are you still awake?" She said as she stuck her head in the door, supporting herself with the door frame.

"Why, yes child, I am. What do you need?"

"I think you better call Missy. It's time."

"Oh, my word...gracious me," Rose said, as she jumped from the bed.

"Are you sure, Hon?"

"If it's not contractions, it's the worst case of indigestion ever. Yes, I'm sure. Plus, I think my water just broke."

Rose grabbed her robe with one hand and the phone with the other. Then, not being able to dial the phone with her hands full, she dropped the robe on the bed and quickly dialed Missy's number. As the phone rang, she put on the robe.

"Answer your phone, Missy Stover. You answer this....Hello, Missy? It's time. Can you come?"

By the time Missy arrived about twenty minutes later, Rose had Evelyn back lying comfortably in bed, munching on a cup of ice. Missy stormed in, a large bag slung over one shoulder.

"How are you doing, Evelyn?"

"Okay at the moment, but the contractions are coming close together. Is that normal?" Missy could hear the edge of apprehension in the young woman's voice.

"Not abnormal. Sometimes if your water breaks early on, it can be followed by closer contractions. Might even mean you'll have a shorter delivery, but that's not always the case. How far apart are the contractions?"

"I've been timing them," Rose replied. "They're between a minute-and-a-half to two minutes."

"Good." Missy set down her satchel next to the bed, and grasped Evelyn's wrist to take her pulse. "It's all going to be okay, Miss Evelyn. God is here in this room as the miracle of life is about to happen. It's one of the reasons I became a midwife to help escort these little souls into this world.

"Your pulse is strong and steady. That's good. Let's take a quick look and see how things are progressing," Missy said as she reached into her bag and pulled out a surgical glove. When Evelyn didn't move, Missy pointed to where the sheets covered her legs. "Down there, sweetie. Let's be sure everything is okay down there."

"Oh. Sorry." Evelyn pulled the covers back and positioned herself so Missy could examine her.

After a moment, Missy raised her head and smiled. "You're dilating nicely. We may get some sleep tonight after all."

But as often is the case, nature had its own timeline, and the hours dragged on. Around five the following morning, after another vaginal exam Missy declared, "It's time. You're well dilated with plenty of room for the baby to come out. I know you've been pushing for several hours. Those have all been practice for what's about to follow.

"When you feel another contraction coming on, I need you to breathe like this — ei, ei, ei, and push really hard. You're about to have a baby. Okay?

A tired and sweaty Evelyn nodded. "I'm just so tired. If I could maybe just take a long nap and then we can resume tomorrow?"

Missy glanced up to see Evelyn trying to smile at her little joke, but just as she did the next contraction started.

"Okay, honey...breath and push, breath and push," and a couple minutes later, "Good girl. Keep it up. I can see the head." A minute more of heavy breathing and pushing ended with a loud and healthy Waaaiiii!

Evelyn laid back with an exhausted yet satisfied look on her face. "What is it?" she whispered.

"Just as you called it. You're the mother of a beautiful baby girl."

As Evelyn dosed off from fatigue after thirteen hours of hard labor, Missy shuffled through her bag pretending to look for something. Then she looked up at Rose.

"Be a dear and go fetch me some hot water and some fresh towels and sheets. I need to clean our new mother up a bit."

Rose nodded, took one final look at her new grandchild, and with a smile still on her tired face, left to fetch the water from the kitchen downstairs. Missy stood at the bedroom door listening to the sound of Rose's steps down the stairs. Once she was satisfied that Rose was completely gone, she resumed the task at hand.

As she reached into her bag, she glanced up to be sure Evelyn was still asleep. She then pulled out the bottle of chloroform and a wad of four-by-four gauze squares. She opened the bottle and poured a healthy dose of the anesthetic onto the sponges. As she slowly brought the sponges to the new mother's face, Evelyn's eyes shot open.

"What are you...?" Evelyn's words were cut off as Missy clamped the chloroform soaked sponges across her mouth and nose. Evelyn's eyes enlarged with fear, reminding Missy of a deer she once saw caught in the headlamps of her car just before she crashed into it going fifty miles an hour.

But Evelyn wasn't a deer. She was a new mother. She suddenly tapped into a reserve of energy that Missy hadn't expected as she kicked and flayed her arms in an attempt to knock the gauze squares away from her face, while at the same time holding her breath.

Evelyn also had one other reserve that Missy hadn't taken into account; special powers the likes of which Missy hadn't seen for many years. Suddenly all the loose objects in the room began to shake, as though in an earthquake. The lamps, the chairs, the numerous knick-knacks that Evelyn and Rose had accumulated over the years and that were displayed on just about every square inch of flat surface—all began to first shake, then rise in the air, as they slowly then with increasing speed began to circle around the room with Missy and Evelyn as their center of gravity.

"What the Hell?" Missy shouted as she clamped down even harder on Evelyn's face and tried to force the young woman to take a breath by pressing on her chest with her own substantial weight.

"Just take a good deep breath, my fine little dear and before you know it you'll be visiting your master in Hades."

But Evelyn refused to breath, even though Missy could tell that she was starting to turn from a bright red from the exertion to a light blue. Meanwhile, the smaller objects picked up speed, and their circuit was growing smaller and smaller as they closed in on Missy.

Now it was her turn to mimic a deer in the headlights as she noticed several of the objects whizzing by her head were hard porcelain figurines with sharp edges.

She waved at them with her left hand as she continued to press her right one onto Evelyn's face pushing her deeper into the feather pillows behind her head.

Just as it looked like several of the knick knacks were going to crash into her head, she grabbed one of the larger ones, a pony from Evelyn's childhood, with her left hand and smashed it against Evelyn's right temple, knocking her unconscious.

As she did so, the rest of the flying debris came crashing to the floor...just as Rose re-entered the room.

"What in God's name is going on here?"

"Oh Rose, thank God you're back. Evelyn just went berserk for no reason. She tried to kill me. It's like she was suddenly possessed. Yes, that's exactly what happened.

"Oh, my dear Rose. I know how you and your family have been cursed through the years, despite your best efforts. I'm afraid it's very clear that Evelyn's soul has been claimed by Satan. Now that you have a granddaughter, we must do everything we can to protect this young soul from the Devil. As much as I hate to have to say it, that will mean separating her from her possessed mother."

Rose looked around the room at the shambles. Chairs were laying on their side. The bookcases with all their books strung on the floor. The large armoire where Evelyn kept most of her clothes had moved over a foot away from the wall where it had originally been.

"Did she do all this?" She waved her arm around to take in the whole mess.

"Yes, I'm afraid she did. Things were flying all over the place. Several of them almost struck me. One of them did hit Evelyn. That's when everything came crashing down proving it was Evelyn who's possessed by a very strong and evil force."

Rose's composure began to crumble as the first tears streaked down her face. She shook her head. "I tried to warn her not to mess with her powers. I tried to tell her they were evil and from the Devil, but she wouldn't listen to me. She was always so sure she could handle them. She just didn't have any idea what she was dealing with."

CHAPTER SIXTEEN
Rose's Confession

NO trumpets sound when the important decisions of our life are made. Destiny is made known silently. Agnes DeMille

AS HERB PLACED THE phone back in its cradle, he turned his attention to his wife who had gotten out of bed and put on her bathrobe. In the over forty years of marriage, he'd never seen her look so distraught or old. Despite her sixty-plus years, Rose had always looked much younger than her age, but this morning she looked years older. He suspected it was more than just that she hadn't had time to put on any makeup.

"What's going on here, and what do you know about it?" He tried to say it firmly but with at least an edge of compassion. After all, they'd been through a tremendous amount over the past forty-plus years. Somehow, they'd get through this too, whatever "this" was.

Rose opened her mouth as though to explain, but all that came out was a cry of anguish as she collapsed to the floor crying.

"Oh, what have I done, what have I done?" She mourned as she crawled to where he was sitting on the edge of the bed.

"Will you ever be able to forgive me for what I have done?" She broke down, throwing her arms around his legs as she knelt in front of him. Herb allowed her to stay in that position for a minute as he gently caressed her gray hair. Finally, he spoke.

"What is it, Rose? If you know where Amberlin is, please you've got to let me know. She could be in danger."

Rose took a couple of deep, jagged breaths, then slowly looked up as she tried to compose herself. She pointed to the box of tissues on his nightstand, and as he reached over for a couple, she glanced down at the notes he'd written during the call. She pointed to one of the lines.

"I think I know what this means," she said, pointing to the words, *trapped vault*.

"What?"

"It can only mean that Amberlin has gone to her mother's vault at the church and has become trapped."

"What on earth would possess her to do something so foolish and at such an hour?" But even as he asked the question, he gently extricated himself from Rose's grasp and walked across the room to where his shirt and pants lay on a chair.

As he put his pants on he looked at his wife. It looked like she was about to break down again, but with a deep sigh and a straightening of her shoulders, she kept her composure.

"Well, that will take some explaining," she said as she walked over to the armoire where she kept her clothes. "We can talk about that on the way over to the church."

"No, you'll tell me now. What have you done to put our granddaughter in such danger?"

Rose sat down on the edge of the bed, looking even more tired and even older than a few minutes before. Finally, she looked up at him and began to talk.

"It happened at the end of Evelyn's delivery when Satan made his appearance."

Herb felt his jaw tighten. Rose knew it was a major difference in their beliefs — whether, in fact, the devil existed or not. They'd finally agreed to disagree and avoided talking about it as much as possible, but he refrained from saying anything.

"She'd just delivered this beautiful baby girl. Missy had sent me downstairs to get a few things so she could clean Evelyn and the baby. When I returned the room looked like a tornado had struck, which according to Missy it had—a tornado from hell."

Herb fought to keep his facial expression as neutral as possible as he finished dressing.

"It was clear to Missy and me that Satan had completely taken possession of Evelyn, so to protect her and Amberlin, Missy recommended a place where Evelyn could get the treatment she needed."

"You mean my daughter is alive?" Herb shouted before he could stop himself.

Rose nodded too ashamed to look him in the eye but instead rushed on with her story.

"We knew if others found out that Evelyn was possessed. It could destroy the whole community. Everything that we'd worked for so many years to build. So, we faked her death and told everyone she'd died in childbirth. It wasn't so much a lie. After all, the Evelyn we'd known was dead."

Rose finally looked at her husband. "I wanted to tell you...really I did, but Missy made me promise to tell no one. It's eaten at my soul ever since. It's long past time I came clean with you on this. Long past time."

Herb stared out the window, stunned by Rose's confession. Finally, realizing that his granddaughter might be in grave danger, he walked to the door. As he opened it, he turned back to his wife. "We're not done talking about this, not by a long shot." He stormed out, slamming the door behind him.

As Papa Herb drove to the church, his white-knuckled hands gripping the steering wheel. Rose's story replayed in his head along with the realization. Evelyn was alive!

He pounded the steering wheel with one hand. How could they have done this to his precious child? Just wait 'til he saw Missy Stover again. But all that would have to wait for now. First, he had to find Amberlin, make sure she was safe, then...why they'd just have to go find her mother. It suddenly occurred to him that it wasn't too late. Maybe he hadn't failed with Evelyn. How was he to know? He had been overseas on that writing junket. How convenient that had turned out to be maybe too convenient.

As he turned into the church parking lot, he glanced at his watch. How long had it been since he'd received that cryptic phone call from...what was her name? He pulled the slip of paper from his shirt pocket. Miriam. He had meant to call her back. Well, that too would have to wait just a little longer.

As expected, the parking lot was empty, but would it remain that way? Something prompted him to park his car in the corner of the lot where it would be less conspicuous. Trouble was afoot tonight. No reason to call more attention to himself than he needed to. He reached across to the glove compartment and pulled out a flashlight.

Suddenly, he was nervous he'd waited too long for Rose to tell her bizarre story. What if Amberlin wasn't okay in that vault? What if she wasn't even there? Maybe Missy or Rev. Stover had taken her somewhere else. After all, how could Miriam have gotten a message from so far away? Then he remembered. Where the Gentry women were concerned, just about anything was within the realm of possibility.

He jogged to the door closest to where the hallway of burial vaults were and was not surprised to find the door unlocked. So, someone has been here, after all, he thought. As he slipped into the church, he flipped the flashlight on but held the beam down just a few feet in front of him. His soft soled deck shoes made almost no noise on the linoleum floor.

Within moments, he was at the vault with Evelyn Gentry's name on it. He put his ear to the door as he tried the handle. Damn! Of course, it was locked, and he'd left the key back at the house in Rose's desk drawer. He pounded on the door with his fist, taking out some of his frustration that way and skinning his knuckles.

"Hello, is anyone in there? Amberlin are you in there? Hello?"

He put his ear to the door again but heard nothing, so he tried pounding and yelling again. This time, when he listened, he heard a soft reply.

"Papa Herb, is that you?"

"Yes, my dear. I'm here. I'm going to get you out. Just hold on."

"She did it. My mother did it. She received my message. She's alive." He could just hear his granddaughter's soft cry on the other side.

"Yes, dear heart, your mother is alive. Now, step back away from the door. I'm not quite sure what may happen next. It's been a long time."

No time to return home for the key, he thought. He could tell from the weakness of his granddaughter's voice that she'd not be alive by the time he returned.

Only one course of action was left to him. He just prayed to God he hadn't completely lost his touch. He braced himself and took several deep breaths, focusing his attention on the key hole just below the handle. He closed his eyes and imagined being a beam of white light traveling into the keyhole. Once well inside, he focused all his energy and attention on expanding the white light...adding more and more energy to that small concentrated area.

First nothing happened, and he began to wonder if indeed it had been too long, but it couldn't be. He had to do this. Amberlin's life depended on it.

He continued to take deep cleansing breaths, then another and another. With each exhalation, he directed more and more energy into the white light until it became as powerful as a laser beam, heating up the old lock mechanism... until finally he felt it start to give away.

He placed his hand firmly on the handle and started to press down on it, waiting for just the right moment, then suddenly he forced all his weight down on the handle. It resisted for an instant, and then the combination of the internal heat and the weight was too much for it. It gave way.

He hadn't lost his touch. The Gentry women were not the only ones with a few tricks up their sleeve. The door swung open a few inches.

"My dear Amberlin," he called. "It's time. We're going to find your mother."

"The hell you are," a stern voice said behind him. He turned to see the large frame of Missy Stover holding a gun pointed straight at his heart. "I should have known you'd be one of the devil's sidekicks."

"So you see my fine brothers and sisters of Christ," Rev. Stover pointed to the pictures being passed around among the twelve members of the Community Council. "The Gentry family has fallen to the temptation of evil forces. We must take definitive action to rid our community of such, just as God cast out Satan from Heaven.

"Thus says the LORD concerning all My wicked neighbors who strike at the inheritance with which I have endowed My people Israel. Behold I am about to uproot them from their land and will uproot the house of Judah from among them." It was one of Stover's favorite Bible quotes he saved for special occasions like this.

"Why this is outrageous!" Jacob Walden shouted as he slapped the photo he was holding in his hand down on the coffee table. "Imagine, right here

among us. The devil is doing its nasty work right under our noses. So very like
him to choose one of our staunchest members to play his evil games. Why,
we can't allow it. We mustn't allow this to go on another minute. We've got
to do something."

Several other members agreed. Rev. Stover smiled to himself. He could
feel the anger building in the room. Walden was following his instructions to
a T. It wouldn't be long now before his flock of sheep would transform into a
pack of wolves and chase the Gentrys from their midst for good.

Missy glared at Papa Herb, then to the smoking lock of the door and
back to him.

"I should have known. You've been taken over by evil just like the rest of
them. I bet you're Satan's ring leader, aren't you? How else would you have
been able to do that?" She pointed to the door with the muzzle of the revolver.

Papa Herb glared back at her. He took a step towards her but stopped
when Missy directed the gun back to this chest. I've got to get her away from
Amberlin, he thought. Somehow distract the old bitty long enough for her
to escape.

"There is no greater evil in the world than the evil that masquerades as
good." He threw the proclamation at her. "You know all about that, don't
you Missy? First, you corrupted Rose, convincing her that her gifts were evil
when the source of the evil wasn't the gifts. It's you."

As he talked, he inched away from the door, the muzzle of Missy's gun
following him as did her attention.

"Then you tried to kill my daughter, didn't you? I suspect you had plans
to kill both of them, but when that didn't work, you banished Evelyn to some
hellhole that masquerades as a mental institution."

He continued to circle away from the vault's door, looking for an opening
to get a jump on her.

"Do you have the nerve to shoot someone facing you, Missy? Or would
you prefer I turn around so you can shoot me in the back? Isn't that more
your style? But then, how will you explain yourself?"

"Shut up, old man. It won't matter where I shoot you because no one is
ever going to find your body."

Papa Herb continued to slide along the wall of the hallway away from the door of the vault, which was now behind Missy.

"Bodies have a strange way of turning up, you know. Seems to have something to do with good over evil. True evil, like the evil that has eaten away at your soul."

As he talked, he noticed the door to the vault slide open, inch by inch. Please, God, help her slip away to safety. Take me if you must but save her. You know she has much good work to finish here on earth.

But as he watched it became evident to him that Amberlin had no intention of slipping away. As she pushed the door open the final couple inches so she could slip out of the vault, he noticed she held something in her right hand. It wasn't until the object came crashing down on Missy's head that he recognized it was Hannah's leg brace.

Ben Junior sat quietly in the straight back chair listening for sounds of life in the rest of the house. At the first signs of movement overhead, he rocked back and force in the chair in an attempt to make as much noise as possible.

Scraping the legs of the chair against the cold concrete floor of the basement was the only noise he could make. His mother, Missy, had "restricted him to his room." Not his regular bedroom upstairs, but to the basement. Forcing him at gunpoint to first tie his legs to the legs of the chair, then tie a strand of rope around one arm so she could finish tying his hands behind his back.

She then finished off by wrapping a piece of duct tape over his mouth. Just like she'd done on numerous occasions before though not in the last couple of years. He had thought she'd grown out of the practice, or more accurately, he thought he'd grown up too much for her to be able to get away with it. Unfortunately, today's extenuating circumstances called for her drastic measures.

In earlier days, starting around when he was three, it had taken next to nothing for him to end up with a long stay in "his room."

"Ben Stover, I've had it with you. Every time your father leaves on one of his damn trips you think it gives you free license to act out and ignore my rules. Well, I won't have it, you hear. I won't have it!"

Four-year-old Ben stood petrified between his mother's strong arms, one on each of his shoulder, as she shook him on each word to drive her point home.

"I'm soorrryyy," his voice vibrated partly from the shaking and partly from the fear. "I'll try to behave."

"Too late for that," Missy shook him one final time then started dragging him down the hall, not stopping until they were in front of the door that led to the dark and dank basement.

"Noooo, not there, mom. Pleeasse...dark—too dark. I'll be good," Ben pleaded, but his words seemed only to anger his mother more. She opened the door and dragged her son down the steps. At the bottom, she reached over her head until she found the cord that turned on the single light—a bare bulb that hung from the rafters.

The light partially illuminated the unfinished basement, revealing a lone, straight back chair in the middle of it.

"This is for your own good," Missy said as she pushed him into the chair. "You've got to remember to follow the rules. God's rules and my rules, you understand?"

"I will...I'll do better, promise. Please don't leave me down here again."

"Easy words for you to say, but obviously from your actions today, not nearly so easy to follow." Missy, pulled out the ropes that laid at the chair's feet, and began to secure her son's feet to the chair legs. "You sit down here and pray for forgiveness and think about how you can keep that promise to your mother."

Finished with securing his legs, she pulled his arms behind the back of the chair and secured them there. She stood up and perused her handiwork. "Open your mouth."

"Please, I'll be quiet. Really I will. Please, no..."

But before he could finish his sentence, she stuffed the sock in his mouth and secured it with a piece of duct tape.

"Pray, my son. Pray for forgiveness from God. Then I'll let you figure out how you can convince me to forgive you for your sins and evil ways."

As she started up the stairs, she pulled the cord, turning off the light. She could hear her son's moans and the scraping of the chair as he fought to loosen the ropes until she closed the basement door, and all was quiet.

"Finally, a little peace and quiet before the ladies come over for our Bible study."

He still hated the dark, hated the chaffing of the course rope around his wrist, and the tape over his mouth that made it hard to breathe, even though, thank God, Missy hadn't been able to find anything to wedge in his mouth this time.

He guessed he'd never get used to cold, dark and dank basements, but today was especially bad. He knew if he didn't find some way to get out of there soon, his two friends were going to die, and it would be all his fault.

Which was why he had dared to tie the rope around his left wrist a little loose, then prayed that Missy wouldn't check it too closely. For once, one of his prayers had finally been answered. Now, if he could just slip his hand...out...of....the....loop.

There! The layer of sweat that covered his body had served as lubricant. As Ben ripped the tape from his mouth, he felt the tears well up in his eyes from the pain. He quickly untied his legs, then considered his next move.

The door leading from the basement to the first-floor hallway would almost certainly be locked. Besides, it could be dangerous exiting that way. He might run into one of his parents. But the basement also had a storm door that led to the outside that hadn't been used in years.

That door was locked as well, but the rotten wood gave way on the third time he slammed his shoulder against it. He'd probably have a bruise there by tomorrow. A small price to pay for his freedom.

He thought of trying to retrieve his bike but decided it was too risky, so he set out on foot at a fast jog towards the church.

CHAPTER SEVENTEEN
Fight Fire with Fire

THERE is no such thing as chance; and what seem to us merest accident springs from the deepest source of destiny. Johann Friedrich Von Schiller

IT TOOK LESS THAN TWO hours before the sparks that Rev. Stover had set in the community meeting roared into a full-fledged forest fire. One that grew rapidly out of control beyond what even he, the arsonist who had lit the first match, had anticipated.

Before he knew it, an angry mob of righteously indignant men and women had materialized seemingly from thin air outside the Walden's home, demanding the Gentry family be expelled from Golden Acres.

As the mob mentality took over, it became clear to everyone who took part that simple expulsion was too good for Satan's spies. They needed a clear and demonstrative act that would show Satan that they would not tolerate such evil in their midst.

"It's time to fight fire with fire," brother Walden yelled. "The fire and brimstone of Hell will meet with the righteous fire of God." He held up a can of gasoline he'd retrieved from his shed.

Several others from the committee took up the chant. "Fight fire with fire...fight fire with fire."

Where had Walden come up with that idea? Rev. Stover wondered, growing nervous that the mob was growing out of control, but not knowing what to do about it. Missy had said she wanted the Gentry clan out of Golden Acres once and for all, and for sure burning them out would send a clear and undeniable message.

A couple of the men found a dozen torches in Walden's shed that they'd used for a Hawaiian Luau the previous summer. As the mob continued to grow in number, it started marching down the street towards the Gentry's home.

"I sure hope this is what Missy wanted," Rev. Stover muttered to himself, "'cause there's no way anyone is going to be able to stop it now."

The first thing Rev. Stover noticed as he approached the Gentry's home with the vigilante mob he'd orchestrated was that their automobile was missing from the driveway. Probably just as well, he thought. This thing is starting to get out of hand. Before I know it, someone's likely to be injured. Discrediting someone was one thing. Casting them out of the community, okay. He could live with all that, but one of God's Commandments was "Thou shalt not kill." Okay, sure millions had been killed by religious fanatics through the centuries. He wasn't sure he was ready to step over that line and join them.

Coming home and finding your home burned to the ground, though. That delivered a pretty clear message that you were no longer welcome.

Already Brother Walden was busy emptying his gas can onto the Gentry's porch. Several of his other male congregants stood close by with their lit torches, too close for Stover's comfort. If they're not careful, they're going to catch Brother Walden on fire in the process, he thought. Behind the men with torches, a dozen or so of their wives lined up shouting words of encouragement and Epitaphs from the Old Testament.

"Sinners will have no place among the godly."

"We know where you live—where Satan has his throne."

Then, as Brother Walden stepped back to admire his handiwork, the chanting began again.

"Fight fire with fire! Fight fire with fire!" Then one especially exuberant woman shouted "Fight Satan's fire with the Divine fire from God," and with that she grabbed one of the torches and threw it towards the porch.

As Walden watched the torch arch its way towards him, he realized he was in the direct line of fire, surrounded by gasoline soaked wood, holding an almost empty gas can. Moving faster than Rev. Stover could remember ever seeing Walden or anyone else move, Walden threw the can through the closest window and leaped over the porch railing. He hit the ground and rolled as the porch exploded into a fiery inferno.

Like the rest of the Gentry's home, the porch had been built over fifty years ago from the staunchest oak prolific to the western North Carolina mountains. Over that half century, it had cured to a hard, dry, almost brittle finish that was perfect kindling for a fire. Within minutes, the whole front of the house was in flames.

And the chanting, "Fight fire with fire! " grew in volume as the flames spread.

Rose sat rocking herself back and forth in the rocking chair where she had comforted Evelyn, then later Amberlin whenever they were too colicky to sleep. But she held no baby to her breast this day. She rocked, instead, to find some comfort for herself.

For too many years, she'd withheld these secrets from her husband, and now she realized she'd also walled them away from herself. She had buried them deep within her psyche to protect herself from the truth of what she'd done and allowed others to do to her only child. But the truth was now out in the open, not only to Herb but herself, and it began to streak down her face in the form of tears. Tears that burned her heart with the naked reality of what she'd done, and how it had shaped who she'd become.

I'm a wicked woman, she thought. Evil and no good. To do what I have done to a stranger would be bad enough, but to do it to my own flesh and blood? Pure unadulterated evil! I will burn in Hell for this, and rightly so.

And that's when she heard the shattering of glass downstairs.

Ben Jr. was only a couple blocks from his house when he heard the first sounds of the crowd in the distance that quickly gained in volume as he drew nearer to the Gentry's home.

"Fight fire with fire...fight fire with fire...." As the words became clearer, a shudder of fear passed through him. What is going on now? Could this be happening in Golden Acres? Aren't we supposed to be all about brotherly love and loving our neighbors as ourselves? Typical hypocrisy, he thought as he drew close enough to see what was happening on Amberlin's front lawn.

He'd left his two friends back at the church, locked up in Amberlin mother's crypt. Funny, he thought. That might prove to be one of the safer places to be these days. But what if they'd gotten out somehow and returned to Amberlin's house? They could be in there!

He decided to circle around the house to where he could see the window of Amberlin's bedroom. If the two girls had returned home, then they might still have a light on, he thought. He skirted around to the backyard, being careful to avoid detection by anyone in the crowd. Luckily, everyone appeared mesmerized by the mounting flames anyway.

There wasn't any light on in Amberlin's room, but there did appear to be a one coming from down the hall. That would be her grandparents' room, he thought. Of course, they might still be in the house.

As he continued to watch, he thought he saw some movement coming from the lit room — a shadow moving across the far wall perhaps, but he couldn't be sure. Then suddenly, the silhouette of someone standing before the window looking out appeared for just a moment, then turned and walked off, but in that brief moment of seeing the shadowed profile Ben knew. Rose Gentry was still in the house.

The realization burned in Ben's chest like a severe case of heartburn. What to do? After all, who was this old woman to him? Oh, she'd always treated him nice enough. Never refused him a plate of her cookies or even a second slice of her delicious apple pie, but still. It was Amberlin who was his friend, not her grandmother. It was Amberlin who needed his help, not...but no, they both needed his help. How could he ever hope to look Amberlin in the face knowing that he'd had a chance to save her grandmother's life but had turned away. Hell, how could he ever look at himself in the mirror if he turned away now. Hold on Amberlin. I'll be there in just a few minutes.

Having made up his mind, he ran to the back door, praying it would be unlocked as were most of the doors in Golden Acres. It was. He thought of knocking then realized how silly that would be. Did firemen knock before entering a burning building? He didn't think so. He wasn't that familiar with the house, having spent most of his time in the Sanctuary out back. He stumbled through the rooms bumping into furniture and knocking over unidentified knick knacks that he was sure he'd have to pay for if Mrs. Gentry found out he'd broken them.

Come on, get a grip. The whole house is going up in a blaze. No one is going to bother with a few broken china dolls.

He felt his way to the banister of the stairs. As he started up them, he called out, "Mrs. Gentry...Mrs. Gentry. It's Ben Stover. Are you up there?"

He was halfway up the stairs when a light in the upper hallway came on.

"Ben? What are you doing here this time of night? Amberlin isn't here. She's..."

"Mrs. Gentry. Your house is on fire! We've got to get out of here?"

"My house is what? What did you say?"

He saw her take a few steps down towards him and stop.

"They've set your house on fire. Can't you smell it?" As he asked the question, a whiff of smoke caught in his lungs, and he coughed. He pulled a handkerchief from his back pocket and placed it over his mouth.

"Please, Mrs. Gentry. Come with me. I think we can still get out the back way." But as he glanced around, he wasn't so sure. The fire seemed to be spreading in every direction, and the smoke was growing thicker by the second.

"Oh, no. You go on. I'm not leaving my home. This is God's retribution, and it's well deserved. The sword of the Lord is swift and mighty."

What is she talking about? Has she gone nuts?

"Mrs. Gentry. Please walk this way. I'm here to help. Please let me help you." As he spoke, he ran up the last few stairs separating them and grabbed her arm.

"Ben Stover Junior, you let go of my arm this very minute. How dare you..."

He ignored her admonitions. "Here," he said handing her the handkerchief. "Placed this over your mouth, and stay as low as possible."

He'd remembered the instructions he'd received at school on what to do in the case of a fire. The fire marshal had told them that the smoke was as much a killer as the flames, so the lower you could stay the less dense the hot smoke would be.

Funny, he'd never thought he'd needed to know such trivia, but suddenly the trivia had turned into some of the most important information of his life.

Rose Gentry was crying now. It started as quiet sobs at first then louder, turning into almost wales. "I deserve this. I'm a wicked, evil person. I'm not worth saving...really I'm not," she cried out as Ben continued to drag her towards the kitchen, but it wasn't looking good. Somehow the fire had circled around and was engulfing the back door.

"Listen, you've got to help me," Ben said as he looked around for another way out, but couldn't find one. "You know this house better than I do. Is there another way out other than the front door or the back?

"No," Rose replied, but then paused as though thinking.

"What is it? Mrs. Gentry, please. You may be a terrible, hateful person, but the jury is still out on me. I'm too young to die. If you won't help yourself, at least help me."

"Well, there's the root cellar," Rose finally replied.

At the word, cellar, Ben felt the icy fingers of fear grip his heart. No way he was going down in someone else's cold, dank, and dark basement.

CHAPTER EIGHTEEN
Road Trip

CONTROL your destiny or somebody else will. Jack Welch

AS AMBERLIN HELPED Hanna to her front door, she continued to apologize. "I'm so sorry to get you involved in this and for damaging your brace."

Her friend stopped and smiled. "Are you kidding? This day has been one of the best of my life...certainly one of the most exciting. I wouldn't have missed it for anything. I just wished I could go with you and your grandfather."

"Me too," Amberlin replied, "but he's right. I've gotten you into enough trouble as it is. Are you sure you and your mom will be okay?"

Hannah nodded. "Don't worry about us. We can take care of ourselves. You just find your mom. I look forward to meeting her soon."

The two girls hugged for several seconds, then finally parted company. Back in the car, Amberlin let out a heavy sigh. "I sure hope they'll be okay. "

Papa Herb reached over and patted her knee. "We've got to get some distance from here," he replied. "When we stop to call Miriam, I'll also call the sheriff's department. We'll have them keep an eye on your friends just in case although I imagine Missy will have her hands full for a while."

"What do you mean? Doing what?"

"Trying to stop us from finding your mother."

"Oh, yeah, that," Amberlin replied. "Do you really know where my mother is?"

"I sure do...or at least I have a good idea and know someone who knows exactly where she is."

"Is that this Miriam person?"

"That's right, dear. When we get out of here, I'll find a phone booth and call her for more specifics. In the meantime, try to relax and get some rest. We still have a full day ahead of us."

Amberlin realized that she'd been running on adrenalin for several hours and that indeed she was tired. She eased back into the seat and using her sweater for a pillow leaned her head against the car window. She was asleep in a matter of minutes.

"Ahh, I can't go down there," Ben said as he stared at the trapdoor leading down to the Gentry's root cellar.

"Sure you can," Rose replied. "There are steps down. They're kinda steep, but if I can manage them, I'm sure you can."

"It's not that. You don't understand. It's just that..." But he realized indeed she didn't understand nor was she likely to in the short time they had before the house burned down around them. No, the root cellar might be fine for her, but he'd have to find another way out.

"Okay, you first," he said as he gently pushed Rose forward.

Rose hesitated for just a moment and turned towards him. "That's something I've always like about you, Ben. You've got manners."

She turned and held on to him for support as she started down the steps. When she was just about all the way down, Ben leaned over the hole and yelled down. "I'll be right there. I've got to get something." He started to close the door then stopped. "Mrs. Gentry, no matter what happens, don't open this door."

"What? Ben? What are you going to do?" But he ignored her question and dropped the trapdoor in place. He stared through the smoke and flames looking for something that would help protect the door and keep it and the surrounding flooring from catching on fire. He found a throw rug in the next room. Crawling now on his hands and knees in an effort to avoid the clouds of smoke that were dropping lower, he pulled the rug into the bathroom. He soaked it with water, then dragged it back to the entrance to the cellar.

It's the best I can do, he thought as he looked around at the fiery inferno that he had apparently now condemned himself to. No, don't give up on yourself just yet, he thought. There must be somewhere the fire hasn't reached yet. If I can just find it and get there, maybe I can find a way out.

He glanced around then looked up. Of course, the fire had been started on the ground floor. It probably hadn't reached to the second floor or the attic. Of course, it was only a matter of time, probably a few minutes at best before he'd find himself in the same dilemma. At the moment even a couple of minutes of reprieve from being burned alive looked like the best choice he had.

He crawled back to the stairs that led up to the second story. As he climbed away from the fire, he remembered the oak tree at the far end of the house near Amberlin's bedroom. She'd used it many times when she wanted to pretend to be in bed asleep but had other plans that often included Hannah and him.

If she can manage it, I know I can. He ran towards her bedroom, keeping as low as possible for the smoke was becoming stiflingly thick up here as well. As he opened the bedroom door, he had a moment of discomfort at entering it. He'd never been allowed in his friend's bedroom.

"It's just not proper to have a young man in your room." He could remember hearing Amberlin's grandmother say countless times.

Well, today would be the exception to that rule, he thought as he threw the door open and ran to the window. *Besides, I don't plan to stay here any longer than I need to.* With that, he raised the window at the far end of the room and climbed out.

"Miriam, my dear, what is going on? You're pacing like a tiger trapped in a cage," Mama Winslow asked her daughter. "Why don't you come over here and have some tea and keep your ol' mother company."

Miriam tried to smile to set her mother's mind at ease but failed terribly. It had been well over half of an hour since she'd arrived home and still no call from Mr. Gentry. She'd finally tried calling him back, but the phone just kept ringing, and the longer it rang without an answer, the more apprehensive she grew.

She walked over to the dining room table where her mother had set out tea and biscuits with a jar of her homemade preserves for her daughter.

"If you let me know what happened at work, I just might be able to help," her mother said as she poured her some tea.

Miriam took a couple sips from her cup, blowing over it to cool it, as she considered what to say. Not only what to say, but how much to say and where to start. It had grown undeniably clear to her in the last few hours that the Asylum was little more than a prison. She'd grown to suspect this to be true over the last several weeks. Now, with what she'd learned, there could be no doubt.

"Oh, mother. I don't know quite where to start. It's such a mess, and I'm right in the middle of it."

"Well, my dear sweet girl. I've found the best place to start is at the beginning. Tell me the whole story and let's see where it goes." Mama Winslow patted her daughter's hand. "I'm sure with God's help we can sort it all out."

So Miriam related the full story as best she could, focusing primarily on her relationship with Spooks and what she'd recently learned that morning. When she was finally finished, she felt better, if for no other reason than she no longer felt like she was alone.

Mama Winslow sat for several minutes sipping on her tea before finally saying, "Well, my dear. And all this time I thought God had sent you home to take care of me. It appears I was only part of the reason, and no doubt not the main one either."

"What do you mean?"

"It's very clear to me He sent you home to help this poor woman as well as the rest of those poor souls being kept captive in that horrid place."

"But what am I to do?"

"Well, now, what have I always taught you to do when you don't know what to do?"

Miriam sat with the question for a minute; then a slow smile began to form on her lips. "Ahh, yes. I seem to have momentarily forgotten one of your most important lessons to me. Will you join me?"

"What's that dear?" Mama Winslow played along.

"Will you pray with me?"

"Why, I'd love to dear."

The two women held hands as they bowed their heads.

After the first five minutes of the two of them praying, the phone rang.

The old gray sedan hit the pothole so hard Papa Herb feared it might rupture the tire. "Damn!" he said as he held his breath waiting to hear the flub-dub, flub-dub that would indicate a flat tire, but no such sound ensured.

Amberlin stirred next to him, pulling down the jacket he'd draped over her when he'd stopped to make his calls. "What was that?" Amberlin asked.

"I'm sorry to awaken you so abruptly. These old mountain roads aren't in very good shape I'm afraid."

"Where are we?" She asked as she sat up and looked around.

"We're a few miles outside of Foster Flats," Papa Herb replied, not taking his eyes off the road. He'd been driving steadily for over an hour, and his eyes felt tired as did the rest of his body.

"Where?"

"Foster Flats," Papa Herb repeated. "It's where Miriam lives, and it's the closest town to where she works at a place the locals simply call "The Asylum.""

Amberlin rubbed the sleep out of her eyes. "And that's where my mother is, isn't it?"

"Yes, apparently so," Papa Herb replied. "How did you know?"

Amberlin shrugged. "Just had a feeling."

The two drove along in silence for several minutes, until finally Amberlin asked, "How are we going to get her out of there?"

Papa Herb didn't answer at first but mulled over how best to answer the question. Finally, he decided the best way was to tell his granddaughter the truth.

"My plan is first to meet with Miriam outside the Asylum, and then together she and I will go in and meet the administrator. I believe she said his name was Dr. Allen. I'll simply persuade him that what would be best for Evelyn would be for him to release her to my care. We'll then take her home with us."

Amberlin sat next to him for several seconds as though contemplating his response. "And how do you plan to 'persuade' him?"

Papa Herb patted the side of his leg where he could feel the weight of Missy's revolver. "Oh, not to worry, my dear. Your granddad can be quite persuasive when he wants to be."

They drove on in silence for another fifteen minutes, when Papa Herb suddenly slowed the car down, then turned into a narrow driveway that led into the thick woods common to the area.

"Is this it, Papa Herb?"

"Yes, I'm pretty sure it is. I almost missed it, but Miriam had warned me the sign was hard to see, so I had my eagle eyes on full alert." He smiled at her.

"You and your eagle eyes," she said back chuckling. "What other animals parts do you have?"

He thought about the revolver in his pocket again and started to reply, the sting of the scorpion, but then thought better of it.

"Oh, you know I'm not going to give away all my secrets, not even to you. He pointed off to the right. "There, that must be Nurse Miriam." He straightened his shoulders and ran his fingers through his hair in a vain attempt to comb it.

"Let's go meet your mother, dear heart."

As Ben dropped from the oak tree, he breathed a sigh of relief. That was a close one, he thought as he righted himself and brushed off his pant. Way too close to the fires of hell for his likings.

"Oh my God, what are you doing here? Were you in the Gentry's house?" Ben turned to find his father walking towards him, a concerned look on his face.

Ben thought about lying but then realized he couldn't carry it off. More than likely his father had seen him climbing out of Amber's window and had come over to investigate.

"Yes, I was. I thought maybe someone else was trapped in there so when I saw the fire, I went to investigate."

"And was there?"

Ben hesitated for a split second. Could he trust his father with the truth? He glanced beyond his father to the crowd gathered there. He recognized several faces as being board members of the church. No, his father had undoubtedly had a significant role in all this.

"No, not that I could tell," he replied.

His father walked over and gripped him in a bear hug. "Thank you, God, for sparing my son," he prayed. After holding him for a few more seconds, he stepped back and cleared his throat, obviously embarrassed by the show of affection.

"Okay, well that's good to know," Reverend Stover replied. "Come with me now."

"Where?"

"To find your mother, and then to find out where the Gentrys have gone."

"Father, what is this all about? Who set fire to their house?"

The reverend turned as though to walk off, then paused and turned back to his son.

"God," he replied. "God burned down their house."

"You mean lightning struck it?" Ben asked even though he knew better.

"No, not exactly," his father replied. "It's a long story. Maybe one day I'll tell it to you, but for now, we still have work to do." He turned to walk away.

"I think I'll just stay here. Go back home and get cleaned up. You just..."

"No, you won't," Reverend Stover replied in his 'come to Jesus' voice that left little or no room for discussion. "You will come with me, and you will do as I say. Is that clear?"

"Yes...very," Ben replied. "I just thought..." the words hung in the air. "Never mind." He followed his father back to the mob that had grown surprisingly quiet in the last few minutes as though finally starting to realize just what they had done.

"Walden, I need a car. Can you round one up for me?"

"Sure, Reverend. The Albertson's are just down the street. "I'll get his keys for you."

Within a couple of minutes the two Ben Stovers were on their way to the church, both of them wondering what they were likely to find there.

They found Missy Stover sitting at one of the tables in the church's kitchen holding a bag of frozen peas on the back of her head.

"What happened to you?" Reverend Stover asked as he rushed over to where his wife was sitting and gently removed the bag of peas to inspect her head. "You've got quite a bump there."

"Not nearly the bump he'll have once I track him down," she replied wincing from where her husband had gently touched her head. "Leave it alone."

"Who did this to you?"

"Why, that devil, Herb Gentry. No, wait. He was in front of me. It must have been that she-devil, Amberlin. Somehow she got behind me and conked me on the head. Wouldn't surprise me if she has learned to materialize herself wherever she chooses."

Reverend Stover smiled. "Well, I wouldn't go that far…"

Missy turned on him with an angry look. "Oh, you wouldn't, would you? Well, let me tell you something. It's time you got clear just what and who we're dealing with here. These Gentrys are disciples of Satan. Make no mistake about it." She suddenly realized they were not alone.

"What's he doing here? I thought I left him…never mind where I left him. What's he doing here?"

"I found him climbing out of one of the Gentry's windows as the house was burning to the ground. Thought it best to keep him with us for a while."

"Climbing out the window?" Missy shook her head, then winced from the pain. "You burned their house down?"

"No, we burned their house down. You, me, and the rest of Golden Acres."

Missy took a moment to consider this recent news, a slow smile growing on her face. "Well done," she finally replied. "There may be hope for you yet. Was there anyone left inside?"

"Ben says no. He said that was why he went into the house; to see if anyone was still there."

Missy stared at her son for a close to a minute, a mixture of pride and doubt crossing her face. "Are you sure?"

"As sure as I can be stumbling around in a house filled with smoke and flames. I didn't see anyone."

Missy thought a moment. "I know where Herbert and his granddaughter were, but…how about Rose? Was Rose inside?"

Ben shook his head.

"Then where is she?"

Both Ben and Reverend Stover shrugged.

"Did you check their bedroom?" Reverend Stover asked.

"No," Ben replied. "I couldn't get down there. The smoke and fire were too thick. I called, but no one answered. Maybe she was down there but the smoke had already gotten her. I can't be sure."

"Yeah, maybe so," Missy replied. She held the frozen peas to her head and thought for a moment. "Okay. Let's assume for the moment that Rose Gentry is out of the picture. That leaves Herb and Amberlin, and I know where they're going." She rose from her chair and started for the door. "Let's go."

"Where?" Reverend Stover asked. "Can't we go home now? I have a sermon to prepare."

"No, we can't go home. We still have God's work to do. Consider this trip research for your sermon. It can be on the topic of 'an eye for an eye and a tooth for a tooth.' She smirked. "Yes, that's what you can sermonize about on Sunday. Now let's go. You'll need to drive. My eyesight is still a little foggy."

As the three of them walked down the hall towards the parking lot, Missy suddenly stopped. "Wait a minute. They took my gun. We'll need to get another one."

"They took what?" Ben asked. "What in the world were you doing with a gun?"

Missy turned on him like an irate banshee. "I'm doing God's work and don't you ever forget it. She raised her hand with the frozen peas in it as though about to hit him with them.

Reverend Stover eased himself between his wife and son. "Easy there, my dear. No need to take it out on him." He took her hand and gently lowered it. "Besides, I just happen to have what we need in the desk drawer in my office. You never know who might decide to help themselves to the church's coffers. It's important to be prepared for all manifestations of the Evil One. We'll get it on the way out."

Momentarily placated, Missy returned the peas to the back of her head and started walking towards her husband's office. "Yes, indeed. There may be hope for you yet."

It had been over two hours since Evelyn had slipped her painted message under the door, and still not a word from Miriam. She was sure she'd seen Miriam shortly after she'd sent her the message, but that damn Rankin had intervened. Something must have happened. Either Miriam had never received the message, or if she had, she'd be deterred from checking up on it.

Or perhaps she got it, read it, understood it and is even now taking action on helping my daughter, but even as she thought it, she realized how long a shot that was. No, more likely she never got it, or if she did, she just figured it was the ramblings of a mad woman. After all, she works at the Asylum. She's probably just been playing me along, pretending to care. Acting like she's my friend so that she can analyze me further. She's probably here doing research for some advanced degree. Yeah, right now she and Nurse Rankin are probably having a good laugh over this whole thing. Let's see how much further we can push ol' Spooks until she completely cracks up.

The sobs started slowly, growing from deep down in her gut, from the very core of her being. It felt like her very soul was shattering into a million pieces. Well, good news ladies. It won't be long now before your wishes are fulfilled.

Lying in bed she began to beat her head rhythmically against the wall, lightly at first, then with increasing intensity. She found the physical pain distracted her somewhat from the much more painful emotional angst. She continued that way for several minutes until she finally lost consciousness.

CHAPTER NINETEEN
Rescue

WHAT lies behind us and what lies ahead of us are tiny matters compared to what lives within us. Oliver Wendell Holmes

ROSE SAT HUDDLED IN a corner of the root cellar as her home for over half-a-century burned down above her. The cellar was cold, and the remnants of an old blanket she'd found and draped over her shoulders did little to keep her body temperature intact. She shook uncontrollably, often highlighting a particularly vigorous shake with a whimper.

How has my life spiraled so out of control? She wondered. She'd started out with such a strong calling to be good, to be righteous, to follow in Jesus' footsteps. Then the powers of Satan had started, and she had fallen into temptation. And she'd continued to fall. She had plummeted into one sinful act after another, often in an attempt to do good. She saw that now. How frequently in an attempt to do what she thought was right, she'd done wrong. No, that wasn't exactly true. She'd done what Missy told her was right. It had been Missy that had first pointed out that her powers were from Satan; Missy who had convinced her to do away with Evelyn. Could Herb have been right? Were such powers simply given by God, then left up to the individual to decide of their own free will whether to treat them as a gift or a curse from Satan?

A crash of heavy timbers distracted her from her train of thought as she shied away expecting any minute that the floor joists would give way, and her home would crush her into oblivion. But they held, and slowly the crackling sounds of fire and crashes of fallen debris subsided. Her home was gone, but she was still alive but for what purpose? Had God saved her so he could resume tormenting her, offering her temptation after temptation then laughing each time she tried to do good and ended up screwing it up?

No, she thought. Almost being burned to death had made one thing crystal clear. Her number one mistake had been in listening to Missy Stover, rather than listening to her own heart the source of God's true wisdom and guidance. Never again, she vowed. I may still make mistakes. I may still fall to temptation, but it won't be because I listened to the wrong person. With whatever time I have left, I vow to listen to God's Divine Guidance by following my heart. She wished she had a Bible to place her hand on, but even as she had that thought, she knew God would understand. After all, didn't making that vow leave her with a warm glow of peace and satisfaction? That's the God I'm listening to from now on.

And with that affirmation, Rose Gentry arose from her self-appointed tomb and walked towards the stairs a new woman.

The Albertson's Pontiac spewed clouds of exhaust behind it as it chugged down the mountain roads, its cylinders knocking especially loudly on the steep hills.

"Why in the world would you decide to use the Albertson's car for this trip?" Missy asked from the passenger's seat, checking her bag of peas to see if there was any cold left in it. When she discovered that there wasn't, she opened the window and tossed the bag out. "I don't think they've had this monstrosity checked by a mechanic since they bought it over ten years ago."

"As I told you just a few minutes ago, it was the closest car at hand. I was concerned for your life, so I took what God provided."

"Well, next time be a little more specific with your prayer request, how 'bout it?"

"Are you sure we took the right turn back there?" Reverend Stover asked as much to change the subject as anything. "This doesn't feel right?"

"Well, then it almost certainly is right. If we depended on your sense of direction, we'd probably end up in Valdosta, Georgia instead of Foster Flats. Need I remind you that I'm the one with the sense of direction, not to mention that I grew up in these mountains. That turn we took a few minutes ago will cut a good twenty to thirty minutes off the trip, which should get up to the Asylum just about the same time as the Gentrys. Who knows, if they stop for anything we're likely to beat them there."

From the backseat Ben asked, "The Asylum? Is that where we're going?"

"Not that it's any of your business, but yes, that's where we're headed."

"Why?" Ben asked. "What is it? Who are we going to see?"

"Oh great, here with go with the twenty questions game again, right?" Missy turned in her seat a bit to see her son, but the movement caused her head to hurt that much more, so she turned back around. She raised her voice so that she was nearly yelling her reply. "Let's just say we're going to make sure the disciples of Satan don't rescue one of their own from where we've placed her to keep her away from good Christian folks. That's more than you need to know so don't ask any more questions."

"Yes, ma'am," Ben replied. "Hey look, Bobby Albertson left some of his comic books in here. Great, I've not read these two."

"Oh really? Let me see," Missy asked in her most pleasant voice.

Ben passed them to her. "Any more back there?" she asked.

"Well, yeah, but I'm going to read these two."

"Let me see those also," she replied with an edge or authority to her voice.

Ben passed the remaining two comic books to her. She glanced at the cover of each of them. "Just as I thought; filled with sinful words and pictures. Pure crap," she said as she opened her window and tossed them out. "We must make it a point to speak to Bobbie's parents when we return. I doubt they even know what evil things their son has been filling his mind with."

"Ahh ma, they're just comic books," Ben replied, "and they weren't yours to simply throw away."

"It takes a village to raise a child," Missy replied in her most righteous voice. "Especially when the parents are apparently too busy or unconcerned to do it themselves."

She opened the glove compartment in front of her. "Oh good, I see at least one of the Albertson's has their heart in the right place." She picked up the Bible and handed it back to her son. "Here, read this...out loud so that we might all revel in the words of God."

Evelyn awoke and looked around the bare room that had been her prison for the past decade. The bare light bulb that glared angrily down at her, the pipes that ran across the ceiling and occasionally leaked their tepid water, making her room feel damp and dingy. Her eyes fell on the bucket that served as her latrine, emptied daily; that is when the attendant on duty remembered it or felt like it. Otherwise, it sat there smelling to high heaven, reminding her that she was rotten and worthless.

She threw her legs over the side of her bed and sat up. Enough. She'd had enough of their bullshit. Time to face the truth of her situation. No one was coming for her, and there was no escape from this hellhole. She was doomed to spend the rest of her life stuck in this eight by ten cell, smelling her own waste.

"That's what you think," she muttered out loud, a smug smile beginning to form. "It's time for little ol' Evelyn to take control of her destiny." What had her father called it? Divine destiny? Yes, that was it. Time to take control of her divine destiny. Of course, her plan probably wouldn't meet with ol' Papa Herb's preferences, but he wasn't here. No one from her past was here, so it was up to her to take control herself.

She ran her fingers through her grubby hair. She hadn't washed it in over a week, and it itched like she had fleas, which she wouldn't be surprised if she did. "Well, fleas, you're just going to have to find someone else to feed upon, 'cause I'm out of here."

Having made up her mind, she reached under her mattress and pulled out the latest piece of macramé she'd been working on over the past several days. She'd snuck it back to her room under her shirt. She'd told everyone she was making a planter, but no one cared or took notice. If they had, they would have noticed the knotted material didn't look like any planter anyone had ever seen. Her eyes moved from the finely knotted rope to the pipes above her head. She had everything she needed to take back control of her life...at least the last minute or two that remained before the rope would choke it all out of her, leaving the fleas to fend for themselves.

The plan the three of them devised was simple and direct. As Evelyn's father, Papa Herb planned to walk into the Asylum and demand to visit with his daughter. Miriam would corroborate his story, and they'd use Amberlin as Evelyn's daughter to help melt the tough Nurse Rankin's heart.

Of course, Papa Herb knew this was only plan A, and from what Miriam had shared with him about Nurse Rankin, it probably had a less than 50:50

chance of succeeding. He held plan B in his coat pocket, figuring it had a close to one hundred percent chance of succeeding.

The three of them strolled into the foyer area of the Asylum and approached the nurse's station where they found the head nurse going over the records for the day.

"Nurse Rankin, look who I ran into in the parking lot," Miriam said with as much enthusiasm as she could muster. "This is Mr. Herbert Gentry and his granddaughter, Amberlin. They've come to see Spooks. I mean Evelyn. She's Mr. Gentry's daughter and Amberlin's mother. Isn't this exciting?"

Nurse Rankin glanced up from her work, a look of surprise and suspicion growing on her face. "And what were you doing in the parking lot at this time of the day, Nurse Miriam, when you should be resting in preparation for your evening shift?" She slowly stood, straightening her uniform and adjusting her nurse's cap.

"Oh, Mr. Gentry called me earlier today, and we made arrangements to meet here so I could escort him to see his daughter, so would you kindly let us in?" She pointed to the buzzer that would release the door's lock that led to Spook's wing.

Nurse Rankin walked towards the window that connected the nurse's station with the foyer but made no motion to open the door. "And how do we know this gentleman is who he says he is? Besides, there's nothing on the client in question's record about having any children, so I suspect this is all a fabrication. Given the condition of our patients, we do not have visiting hours and particularly not for a total stranger. I must ask you to leave the premises at once and do not return."

Herb felt the hackles on his back raise. He placed his hand in his pocket and touched the revolver, then decided to give plan A another chance. "Miss Rankin, is it? I am indeed Evelyn Gentry's father. The patient I believe Ms. Mason just alluded to as Spooks. She does have a daughter..." He pointed to Amberlin, "...and I'm only too happy to show you my driver's license to prove I am who I say I am."

"Yes, I'm sure you are," Nurse Rankin replied. "But how will I know that it's not a forgery? It's very strange to me, Mr. Whoever-You-Are, that you would suddenly appear after all these years expecting to see one of our patients. Now, I will ask you once more to leave at once. If you don't leave, I will call on of my attendants to remove you."

Herb glanced over at Miriam, who seemed even more distressed over the situation than he was, but then again, she wasn't aware of a plan B. He smiled at her and shrugged. As he did so, he reached back in his pocket and pulled out the revolver.

"Nurse Rankin, I've been kept in the dark about my daughter's situation for over ten years. I was told and convinced that she died in childbirth delivering Amberlin. Now that I know the truth, neither you nor anyone else will deny me seeing my daughter. Believe me, I am a man of peace, but even peaceful men can be driven to violence. Would you like to test that statement?"

Nurse Rankin's face blanched to the color of her uniform. "No, I think I'll pass on that," she said as she reached over and pushed the buzzer. Miriam opened the door.

"Thank you," Herb said as he continued to point the gun at Nurse Rankin. "Now, I'd like you to accompany us to my daughter's room. If it's locked, which I imagine from what I've heard from Miriam it will be, please be prepared to unlock it. Now let's go."

As the four of them strolled down the hall, Herb placed the gun back in his pocket but kept it pointed on Nurse Rankin.

"Nurse Miriam. I hope you realize this will cost you your job," Rankin said as she led them down the hallway.

"Yes, you can consider this my unique way of tendering my resignation," Miriam replied.

Evelyn stepped onto her bed and placed one hand on the wall to steady herself. Once she had regained her balance, she took the rope in her other hand and threw one end towards the closest pipe. It fell short, so she tried it again, then again. The rope passed over the pipe on her sixth try. She reached out to grab the end but it was a foot beyond her reach, so she took careful aim as she leaped off the bed and grabbed it.

Now on the floor, she tested the strength of the rope and pipes by twisting the two ends of the rope together. She then reached up as high as she could, grabbed the rope and lifted her feet from the ground. She felt and heard a groan from the ancient pipes, but they held firm. Firm enough for her needs.

Still holding the rope ends, she stepped back on the bed. She now had plenty of play in the rope to create a makeshift hangman's noose that she then fitted over her head and around her neck. Perfect, she thought as she tightened the noose. It fits perfectly. I guess I'll be the only living thing that sets in this particular planter...and that for only a few seconds longer.

She continued to stand on her bed for several seconds with her eyes closed. She'd stopped believing in the power of prayers years ago, but still, it felt right to say something in the moment.

"Dear Heavenly Father, who, like everyone else, has abandoned me to this hellhole of an asylum, I release my soul to your care." And with that, she took a final breath of life and stepped off the bed.

Papa Herb followed the two nurses down the hall with Amberlin gripping his hand beside him, her knapsack slung over her back. He thought he heard a strange thump followed immediately with a deep gnashing of strained metal.

"What was that?" he asked looking around.

"I don't know," Miriam answered, "but it appears to have come from one of the rooms."

The two looked at each other, both realizing the sound had felt strangely ominous.

"Here we are," Nurse Rankin said as she pointed to the next to the last door along the hallway. "Spooks' room."

"I brought my keys," Miriam said stepping forth to unlock the door. She paused for a moment to look through the small window as she'd learned on her first day of training. "Oh my God!" she screamed as she hastily started to unlock the door.

"What is it?" Herb asked, feeling razor blades of fear cutting through him.

"It's Spooks...she's..." But she couldn't finish the statement. The door wouldn't open. Spooks was on the other side hanging from the ceiling, and she couldn't get the damn door to open. Then she remembered the trick to opening it. She lifted up on the door handle as she twisted the key, and this time the lock released.

As she swung the door open, she rushed over to Spooks, who was swinging like a pendulum from the pipe. "Help me," she cried as she grabbed

Spooks around the legs and tried to lift her up to relieve some of the pressure on Spook's neck.

Papa Herb stood in the doorway, momentarily frozen by the spectacle of his daughter who he'd not seen in over a decade hanging in front of him. But the second passed quickly. Taking in the scene, he knew what he needed to do.

The two nurses were now lifting Spooks up towards the ceiling creating just enough slack in the knitted rope to allow Spooks a little breathing room. Papa Herb focused all his attention and intention on a couple inches of the rope near the pipe. Taking a few deep breaths, he prayed his neglected powers would work just one more time.

They did.

The rope smoldered for a few seconds then caught on fire, and fell from the pipes. Miriam and Nurse Rankin slowly lifted Spooks down and laid her gently on the bed.

Miriam pulled the rope from around her neck, checking for a pulse as Papa Herb and Amberlin stood anxiously awaiting the verdict. The look on Miriam's face communicated their worst fears even before she said, "We're too late."

Amberlin stared down at the young woman's face. It was the same face she'd seen in her dreams over the past several months. It can't be, she thought as the fear gripped her heart, threatening to squeeze it until it exploded. I can't have finally found my mother after all these years, only to lose her in the next moment. God couldn't be so cruel; could she?

But as she continued to stare at the placid, even peaceful look on her mother's face, she feared perhaps God was that cruel, even vindictive. She remembered the many stories in the Old Testament that revealed how arbitrary God could be.

As Amberlin stood there, the tears beginning to well up in her eyes, Miriam placed her chest to Spook's chest, but after several seconds shook her head again.

Suddenly Amberlin found herself stepping forward. Placing her hand on Miriam's, she said, "May I?"

Miriam stared at her a moment, a quizzical look on her face, then stepped back. Amberlin took a step forward and placed one hand on her mother's forehead and another on her chest. As she did so, she closed her eyes and tried to relax. As she took a few deep, cleansing breaths, she gently released the fear that had her heart in such a vise-like grip. She then made a conscious effort to connect with the love she felt for the woman in her dreams; the woman who now lay as though asleep in front of her.

At first nothing happened, but as she continued to breath and release, breath and release, she thought she felt a flutter beneath her hand that lay on her mother's chest, no stronger than the flutter of a butterfly's wing, but something...right? There'd been something there. Perhaps it had been there all along, but until she finally relaxed and became fully present to all her senses, she'd missed it.

Whatever it was, she held onto it, gently at first, imagining she was holding a fragile hummingbird in her hands. She then began to infuse it with the energy of her breath, picturing herself giving her breath over to the tiny bird. She continued this way for, what felt like several minutes though, in truth, all sense of time had drifted away.

Slowly, almost imperceptibly at first, she felt the flutter grow stronger. She continued the process until she felt another sensation...a subtle movement beneath her hand. Had that been a breath? Please, God, let that have been a breath of life. She held both sensations in her awareness as she continued to breathe the love she held for her mother...the woman who had given her life, she was now giving some of that life energy back to her.

Finally, when Amberlin felt she couldn't continue any longer for fear she would be dragged into the darkness herself, Spooks took a breath — a full inhalation of life-giving air. With that, the flutter of a butterfly wing turned into a thready lub-dub of a heartbeat.

Amberlin collapsed to her knees and lost consciousness.

CHAPTER TWENTY
Savior

OUR problems are man-made, therefore they may be solved by man. No problem of human destiny is beyond human beings. John F. Kennedy

AS THE BLACK CLOUDS slowly cleared, Amberlin opened her eyes to find an anxious Papa Herb staring down at her, his large hands gripping hers.

"Come back to us, dear heart," he whispered to her. "She's waking up." He turned and smiled at the others circled around them. "You did it. You really did it."

What had she done, Amberlin wondered, her mind slow to comprehend where she was? She clearly wasn't at home since the only face she recognized was Papa Herb's. She felt one of his hands release hers, then felt it gently beneath her head, helping her to sit up. As the dizziness cleared, she was able to look around, and as she did so, she remembered where she was. They'd come here to the Asylum to find her mother.

Mother! As the word crystallized in her mind, an image of her mother hanging from the very same pipes came into her blurry vision. She could also remember hearing a woman's voice say, "We're too late." Her mother had killed herself, and they'd been too late to stop it. Or had they?

She gazed around her, still partially out of it until her eyes fell on the woman lying on the bed at eye level with her. The woman...her mother had her eyes open and appeared fine. Well, fine might be an overstatement, but at least she looked as well as Amberlin felt, which wasn't saying much.

"You did it, sweetheart," Papa Herb repeated. "You saved my dear Evelyn...brought her back from the brink of death." He turned to one of the other ladies dressed in white. What had her name been? Nurse something-or-other. Did it really matter?

"I'm taking my daughter out of here and back home where she belongs. I'll need a wheelchair."

"I'll get one," the younger nurse replied. Miriam; that was her name. Amberlin remembered she'd been the one that had helped them find her mother.

In a few minutes, once Miriam had returned with the wheelchair, and they'd helped Evelyn into it, Papa Herb leaned down to her. "I'm going to carry you, okay? We're all going home where we belong."

Amberlin nodded, "That would be good. I'm not sure I can walk just yet." She held out her arms as Papa Herb reached down and picked her up. "Let's go home." She reached out and touched her mother's hair. "We're taking you home too."

Evelyn smiled weakly back and with a raspy whisper replied, "It'll be good to be home."

Rose stayed in the cellar for hours, napping at times, praying whenever she was awake. When she finally thought it might be safe to leave, she climbed the stairs and pressed her shoulder against the trap door, but couldn't open it. Great, she thought. Survived my house burning down around me only to die trapped here in my root cellar.

The old Rose might have accepted that, walked back down the stairs and waited while she continued to pray for someone to find her. But not this time. She remembered something her husband had once told her.

"The Quakers have a saying, 'as you pray move your feet.'"

"Well, I'm ready to move my feet," she muttered to herself. She wedged her frail frame between the stairs and the door and heaved...and the door moved though not much at first. She took a deep breath and heaved again and again until finally the debris lying on the door fell to the side, and she was able to open it enough to crawl to the surface.

There she found a light rain had started, soaking the burned out rubble that had been her family's home for most of her life. Her tears mixed with the rain that fell on her smudged face. Despite the tremendous loss, she knelt among the remains and gave thanks.

"...And thank you, Lord, for bringing young Ben to me." As she said it, she wondered, had he escaped or was one of the many charred masses around her all that remained of him? "Please, Heavenly Father, wherever he is, look after the young boy, and guide him to a righteous life." She paused for a moment of silence, checking in with herself to see if there was any postscript she wanted to add. When nothing came to her, she ended the prayer and slowly opened her eyes.

"Now what?" she mumbled to herself. Find your family, came the reply. That's right. Maybe she'd lost her home...not just her physical home but also her community. It was obvious that someone had intentionally set the fire. She remembered hearing the breaking of the window as someone threw something through it, followed shortly after with the first whiffs of smoke. Then Ben had appeared, like an angel sent from above.

No, the fire was a clear sign that she was no longer welcome in the community that had been founded by her father. So be it, she thought. I still have my family. But where are they? Where could Herb and Amberlin be? She thought about it for a moment. Herb had left shortly before the fire started. Where had he gone? To find Amberlin, the answer came. But where...slowly it all came back to her. The strange phone call in the middle of the night. Herb confronting her...her confession. The look of hurt and betrayal that had been on his face.

He's left me, she thought. He'll never forgive me for what I did to our daughter. Can't say that I blame him. Then it dawned on her where Herb and Amberlin probably were. "They've gone to find Evelyn," she whispered to herself. A warm glow suddenly surrounded her. Surely that's where they had gone. They'll be back. And when they return she'd do whatever necessary to make it up to them, even if it took her the rest of her life to atone for her sins.

She looked around. It was almost dawn, but it looked like the rain had settled in for the day. What was she to do until her family returned; if they returned? Where was she to go? She'd lost everything. She wore the only clothes she owned. Herb had taken the car, so she didn't even have transportation. She glanced at the trapdoor that was still partially open. Well, she hadn't lost everything. The root cellar was filled with canned goods and dried meats. At least she wouldn't starve.

She shuddered as the rain began to soak into her clothes. Can't stay out here, she thought. She crawled the few feet to the trapdoor and climbed back down the stairs, pulling the door closed behind her.

After depositing Nurse Rankin in a storage closet that they could lock and making sure she had no keys hidden on her, the four of them headed towards the exit. As they rounded a corner, they ran smack into Jeremy, who had finished his work on the west wing and was heading to the east wing to look in on the patients there.

Everyone stopped, unsure what to do. Carrying Amberlin in his arms made it almost impossible for Papa Herb to reach the gun stashed away in his coat pocket. Before he could move to let Amberlin down, Miriam stepped forward.

"Good morning, Jeremy," she said with the most gracious smile she could muster.

"Morning, Nurse Miriam," Jeremy replied, a confused look on his face. "What's going on here? Who are these people?" He nodded towards Papa Herb and Amberlin.

Miriam decided to use another one of her mother's truisms — honesty is the best policy. "They're Spook's family," she replied continuing to smile warmly. "This is her father and daughter. Isn't it wonderful they've come to visit."

Jeremy nodded, even though the look on his face said otherwise. "I didn't think we allowed visitors?"

"Oh, I know. This is an exception." Miriam could feel her confidence waning as well as her smile.

"Does Nurse Rankin know about this?"

"Why, of course, she does. She's down the hall seeing some of the patients if you'd like to check with her."

Jeremy considered her response for a moment then shook his head. "No, ma'am, I think the less I know about this, the better. In fact, I don't remember even seeing you this morning. No, I think I'll just take a break and have myself a cigarette if it's all the same to you."

"That's probably a good idea," Miriam replied as she sighed with relief. "And Jeremy? Thanks. Thanks a lot."

"No trouble...no trouble at all."

After he had disappeared down the hall, Papa Herb adjusted Amberlin in his arms. "That was a close one."

"I'll say. Let's pray that everything else goes smoothly from here on," Miriam replied as they started towards the exit. "I've had more than enough excitement for one day."

"You can say that again," Papa Herb said, and in a minute added, "There's the front door." He leaned down to Evelyn. "Our car is just on the other side of those doors. We'll be driving home in just a couple minutes."

Evelyn nodded and smiled weakly, and Amberlin squeezed him a little tighter.

Despite all the excitement, Amberlin felt so warm and secure in her grandfather's arms that she began to nod off. It had been a very trying and tiring twenty-four hours. She imagined what it would feel like to be back home in her bed, especially knowing that her mother was in the next room. Shoot, if I'm going to dream, why not have my mother lying next to me, she thought. Liking that picture even better, she sighed and placed her head on Papa Herb's shoulder.

But the chilly morning air slapped her awake as their little entourage left the building that had been her mother's prison for over ten years. They were only a few yards from the cars when she heard a scuffling sound behind them, followed by an all too familiar voice.

"That will be quite far enough," Missy Stover said. "Visiting hours are over."

Papa Herb turned abruptly, and the two of them found Missy and Rev. Stover standing behind them. A few feet behind them stood their son, Ben. But the most dramatic detail of the whole picture that Amberlin couldn't seem to take her eyes off was the snub-nose revolver clutched in Rev. Stover's hand pointed directly at her and Papa Herb.

She felt Papa Herb try to reach for something in his coat pocket, but her leg blocked him from gaining access to it.

"I have to put you down," he whispered to her even as he gave her a final hug and placed her on the ground next to the wheelchair. She stumbled for a moment, her legs threatening not to hold her, but then she grabbed one of the handles of the wheelchair to steady herself.

"That's enough. One more move, Herb, and my husband will have the unique pleasure of shooting one of his congregants," Missy said as she walked over to him and frisked his pockets.

"Well, what do we have here?" She reached into his coat pocket and brought out a matching snub-nose revolver. "Paybacks are hell," she said as she smacked the gun against Papa Herb's head. He fell like a limp dishrag.

"Papa Herb!" Amberlin yelled as she rushed to him. "You leave him alone," she shouted at Missy who simply smiled smugly back at her.

"Now that I have everyone's attention, here's what you're going to do. You're going to turn yourselves around and return to the asylum where we're going to redeposit this poor sick woman back in her room where she belongs. Then I'm going to have to figure out what to do with the rest of you. Might be time to admit the whole lot of you as patients. Now help him up and let's get a move on it." She pointed to Papa Herb with the gun.

Amberlin reached down to help her grandfather up though as weak as she felt, she didn't know if she could make much of a difference. Papa Herb managed a small smile through the pain etched on his face. He had just about reached his feet when all hell broke loose.

He stumbled towards Missy, slamming into her as he grabbed the arm holding the gun. The next second, Amberlin heard two loud gunshots going off almost simultaneously. She felt the air from the bullet of Missy's gun whiz by her ear. At the same moment, she heard a loud yelp of pain from behind her, as she watched a small, rapidly growing spot of crimson appear on Papa Herb's chest.

A look of astonished pain appeared on his face as he slowly sank to his knees, but not before wrenching the gun from Missy's hand. It flew through the air to land on the ground a few feet from Ben, still smoking.

Amberlin turned towards Miriam, shouting, "He's been shot," but Miriam had her hands full trying to staunch the blood coming from Evelyn's shoulder.

Oh, dear God, I can't lose both my mother and Papa Herb, Amberlin thought as she ran to her grandfather's aid. She stooped down to him and pressed her hands against his chest in a vain effort to keep his lifeblood from seeping out on the pavement. Papa Herb tried to smile at her through the mask of pain on his face. He motioned for her to come closer.

As she did so, he whispered, "Remember, I am always with you." They were Herb Gentry's last words.

To Missy, everything seemed to move in slow motion, as Herb Gentry fell to the pavement, shot through the heart by Reverend Stover, who stood with a shocked look on his face. Amberlin rushed to her grandfather, and Miriam attended to Evelyn's shoulder wound — the result of a stray bullet from Missy's gun.

Everyone was shocked by the sudden outburst of violence. Luckily for Missy, she was always able to respond quickly in such situations. Even as everyone else seemed frozen in place or moving as though through molasses, she moved quickly to recover the gun Herb had wrench from her grasp.

Unfortunately, when she went to pick it up from where it had landed on the ground, it was no longer there.

"Back off," Ben yelled at her as he straightened up with the gun in his hand. "Just back off," he repeated and punched the air with the revolver for emphasis.

"Careful, son, that gun is loaded and dangerous." Missy took a step towards him.

"I can see that," Ben replied, then cocked the hammer for emphasis. "And I said to back off, and I meant it."

Missy froze.

"You were right about something you said just a minute ago," Ben replied in a slightly calmer voice. "Paybacks are hell, and now it's your turn to be paid back for all those hours and hours you locked me in that dingy, dark cellar, not to mention all the other godawful things you've put me through in the name of Jesus no less."

He looked over where his father still stood frozen by the shock of having just shot a man. Continuing to point the gun at Missy he called to his father. "Drop it before you shoot someone else."

Rev. Stover shook himself, then glanced at his son. Quickly assessing the situation, he dropped the gun. "Now, son, don't do anything foolish. After all, we are family."

"Don't remind me," Ben replied. He glanced towards Miriam, who was bent over Papa Herb. "How is he?"

"I'm afraid he's dead," Miriam replied softly.

"Oh God," Ben said. "I'm so sorry Amberlin. I really liked your grandpa."

Amberlin didn't respond but continued to sob over Papa Herb's body.

Finally, Ben turned to Miriam. "Do you have a car?"

"Yes," she said pointing to the Chevy.

"I think you need to take Amberlin and her mother to the hospital. You can send someone from there to take care of Mr. Gentry."

"What will you do?" Miriam asked.

"I'll stay here and keep these two from interfering any further."

"We can't just leave him lying here," Amberlin cried. "There must be something we can do."

"I'm afraid not, dear," Miriam said. "The best we can do for him is to take care of his daughter, your mother. We need to get her to a doctor."

Amberlin looked over to where Evelyn was holding a makeshift bandage Miriam had made from her sweater. She slowly nodded. "Yes, you're right."

Miriam went to her car and pulled an old blanket from the trunk and placed it over Papa Herb's cooling body. She also took the first aid kit she kept in the trunk and bandaged Evelyn's wound as Ben continued to watch over his parents.

They were about to leave when Evelyn stopped. "Roll me over there," she instructed Miriam pointing towards where Rev. Stover stood. Miriam did as she was instructed. Evelyn glared at him, and then, wincing in pain from the effort bent down and picked up the gun where he'd dropped it.

"You won't be needing this," she said. "May you burn in hell for what you did today." She looked up to Miriam. "Can you get me out of here now. If I look at him much longer, I think I'll puke."

Miriam and Amberlin helped Evelyn into the passenger side of Miriam's car, and the three of them drove off.

After the Chevy had disappeared down the road, Missy Stover let out a heavy sigh. "Okay, Ben. Now, what are you going to do?"

Ben hesitated. Truth was he didn't have an idea. He'd been making it up as he went, ever since he saw the gun fall at his feet, but he wasn't ready to let his parents know he didn't have a plan.

"Never you mind," he replied. "For starters, we're going to wait here until the ambulance comes from the hospital."

"Really?" Missy replied. "You know, don't you, that it won't be coming alone."

"What?" Ben asked.

"Well, there's been a double shooting here," Missy continued. "You gotta know the hospital will call the police which means the ambulance will be here along with a bunch of police."

"So?" Ben said, not sure what his mother's point was.

"Well, Ben, you're father just shot and killed a man. The police don't take too kindly to such things, you know. That means they'll arrest him...me too since I accidentally shot Evelyn. That'll leave you without any parents to look after you. Do you know what the social service system is around here? Well, I'll tell you. It's not good—not good at all.

"Yep, you'll be finding yourself in a juvenile home before you know it." She shook her head. "It's really too bad because it doesn't have to be that way."

She paused, a smug look of satisfaction on her face. What am I to do? Ben wondered. The thought of being raised in a foster home made him a little sick.

Finally, his mother continued. "If I might make a suggestion?"

Ben nodded.

"Well, we're all family here, and families stick together in a crisis like this. Oh, I know we've had our ups and downs. All families do...even good Christian families, but when the chips are down, we look out for one another, right?"

Ben slowly nodded. "Yeah, I guess...maybe."

"So listen, son, you've done your job. You've helped your friend get away. Now, it's time to let us adults take care of things. Together, as a family, we can get through this." She reached for the gun, but Ben stepped back.

"Not so fast," he replied.

Missy smiled her most loving motherly smile. "I can get us out of this if you'll only let me. There's no reason for any of us to have to go to jail or for you to end up in juvie."

"How?" Ben asked.

"Well, it starts by you trusting me," Missy replied. "It's a little hard for me to think clearly when you're pointing a gun at me. So, give me the gun and I'll tell you my plan." She held her hand out and waited.

Finally, after close to a minute, Ben shrugged. "Guess I'm not all that interested in being a part of the social service system." He handed Missy the gun.

As Missy grasped the gun in her hand, she glared at him and raised it up as though to hit him with it, but at the last moment changed her mind. Instead, as she slowly released the hammer, she laid out her plan.

"Okay, we only have a few minutes until the police get here, so both of you listen and listen closely." She glared at them to be sure they were paying attention. "Your father didn't shoot anyone."

"But he did..." Ben started, pointing to the blanket covered corpse, but stopped when Missy held up her hand for silence.

"No, he didn't," Missy replied. "Crazy Evelyn Gentry shot her own father in retaliation for his committing her to this nuthouse for all those years. You're father, the most caring, compassionate and brave preacher around, tried to stop her but was unsuccessful."

"But the gun..." Reverend Stover started, then stopped. "Right. She has the gun, and it has her prints on it now. Yes, this could work."

"It will work," Missy replied vehemently. "Now, you get yourself in there and wash your hands well. I don't want any power residue to mess up my story. Then get back out here before the police and ambulance arrive.

"Now move — both of you!"

CHAPTER TWENTY-ONE
Picking Up the Pieces

EVERY individual has a place to fill in the world, and is important, in some respect, whether he chooses to be so or not. Nathaniel Hawthorne

IT WAS ALMOST NOON before the rain finally stopped long enough for anyone to investigate the burned out remains of the Gentry's home. Hearing someone sifting through the wreckage above her, Rose finally awoke from her nap. She felt strangely like a troll from one of the fairy tales she occasionally read to Amberlin. "Who's crossing over my bridge?" she muttered as she slowly rose, groaned, and tried to stretch out the kinks from a night no woman in her sixties should ever have to live through.

But I'm still alive, she thought. I'm not sure whether that's a blessing or a curse, but for sure it's a fact. She slowly made her way up the stairs, praying that no one had inadvertently blocked the trapdoor. She breathed a sigh of relief when it opened easily. "Oh, thank you, Jesus."

Tabatha James shouted. "Rose, you're alive!"

Rose was surprised to find she was actually happy to see her old neighbor. They'd never had much use for each other in the past, simply exchanging pleasantries whenever their paths crossed. Just goes to prove what a horrendous night it's been, that I would be glad to see her, Rose thought as she slowly walked towards Tabatha.

"I must find my family," Rose said, almost sounding like the take-control-woman she'd been in the past. "I have to find Herb and Amberlin. I have to make it all up to them somehow."

"Oh my poor, poor dear," Tabatha said as she draped her shawl over Rose's shoulders. "I don't quite know how to tell you this. Perhaps you should come home with me. Let me get you something to eat and drink..."

"Tell me what?" Rose said. She tried to straighten her back and shoulders to show that she was able to handle more bad news though in truth she wasn't sure she was. It didn't matter. Her back protested too much to allow her to pretend to be strong.

"Oh, dear." Tabatha hesitated, looking around, hoping someone else would suddenly appear to help her. When no one did, she continued. "I'm afraid there was a report on the radio this morning of a shooting in the next county."

"Why, what does that have to do with me?" Rose asked, momentarily relieved that it was news that didn't concern her.

"They said the man who had been shot and killed was Mr. Herbert Gentry. Witnesses reported he was shot by his daughter, Evelyn Gentry. But you know how mixed up the news is around here. They can't be right, can they? I mean, Evelyn died in childbirth, so who knows, maybe they got the victim's name wrong as well."

Rose felt like she was about to collapse. She probably would if it hadn't been for Tabatha continuing to hold her. "No," she replied. "I'm afraid the news is right for once." And I'm now a widow.

As the Chevy pulled onto the main road from the Asylum's driveway, Amberlin leaned forward from the backseat as she tried to make sense of the last hour of her life. She remembered Papa Herb telling her once that as most people go through life they rarely realize those pivotal, life-changing moments. However, once in a while something so dramatic happens that you realize your life will never be the same. After such a pivotal moment, life may be much better or much worse, but for sure it would be radically different.

Amberlin felt like the last hour or two of her life had been a series of such moments. In that time, she'd not only discovered that the mother she thought had died giving birth to her was still alive. On top of that, they'd finally been re-united but not until she had to pull her mom back from the edge of death. All that was left was to help her mother escape the insane asylum where she'd been held prisoner for the past twelve years. All good stuff, right?

But on the other hand, she'd also just witnessed the brutal murder of her beloved grandfather who'd sworn to prepare and protect her, not to mention her mother being seriously wounded as well. Bad stuff, no?

"Where are we going?" She asked, not knowing what else to ask but feeling like she needed to talk to keep from going completely loony. She looked first to the pained-streaked face of her mother then to Miriam.

"We've got to get your mother to the hospital. My temporary bandage appears to have stopped the bleeding for the moment, but the bullet is still in her. It has to come out, or it could lead to infection and blood poisoning."

Amberlin stared at the strange woman sitting in the front seat. Strange, and yet not so strange. She felt like she knew her from the steady stream of dreams in which she'd appeared, and yet here she was in the flesh.

She remembered a story Papa Herb once shared with her about an old Cherokee teaching his grandson about life, much as Papa Herb was teaching her.

"A fight is going on inside me," he said to his grandson, "and it's between two wolves. One is evil," the grandfather continued. "He is anger, envy, sorrow, regret, greed, arrogance, self-pity, guilt, resentment, inferiority, lies, false pride, superiority, and ego."

He paused to gaze into the young boy's eyes. "The other wolf is good. He is joy, peace, love, hope, serenity, humility, kindness, benevolence, empathy, generosity, truth, compassion, and faith. The same fight is going on inside you and inside every other person, too."

The grandson thought about it for a minute, waiting for his grandfather to continue. When it was evident that he was done, he asked, "But Grandfather, which wolf will win?"

The old Cherokee smiled. "The one you feed."

Amberlin could feel the evil wolf trying to eat her up with sadness, anger and fear over what had happened to Papa Herb, her mother and her. But there's another wolf inside me as well, she thought, and I get to decide which one to feed. But trying to ignore what had happened to Papa Herb didn't feel right either. It felt, somehow, disrespectful to him, not to mention virtually impossible to forget.

Honor me by giving sanctuary to both wolves, while feeding the one that will enhance your life.

That sounded just like something Papa Herb would have said if he'd been here. A shudder climbed along her back, bringing her back to the present.

"Does it hurt a lot?" Amberlin asked, then after a moment of hesitation added, "Mother?"

"Only when I breathe." Evelyn tried turning to smile at her daughter, but the movement was too painful. "Unfortunately, it's a habit I've found hard to kick."

Well, you almost found a way to kick it, Amberlin started to say but caught herself. There's the evil wolf again.

Turn the radio on, Amberlin.

Where had that thought come from, she wondered, and since when did she start referring to herself in that way?

Please turn the radio on...now!

"Ahh, could you turn the radio on, Nurse Miriam?"

"Sure, honey," Miriam replied. "And you can just call me Miriam. I don't have my nursing job anymore." She reached over and turned on the radio. "Any particular music you like?"

Before Amberlin could answer, she heard the voice of a radio announcer cut into the music.

"We have a special report just in. There's been a multiple shooting at the Western Carolina Sanitarium. The report just released by the Foster Flat Police Department says a man by the name of Mr. Herbert Gentry was shot and killed at the Sanitarium a short time ago. According to eyewitnesses, the man was shot by his estranged daughter, Evelyn Gentry, who had been a patient there. It was reported the shooter was angered by her father for having committed her to the mental institution over a decade ago. She escaped the scene in a light blue Chevrolet, taking a nurse and young child as hostages. She's armed and considered dangerous."

"Oh my God," Amberlin nearly shouted. "That's not what happened. How could they have gotten the facts so wrong?"

"Missy and Reverend Stover," Evelyn replied. "They and their son, Ben, were the only eye witnesses left to give the report." And then a moment later, "Damn."

"What?" Miriam asked.

Evelyn pointed to the gun on the seat between them. "I picked up the murder weapon, and it has my prints all over it. We're screwed."

"Spooks…I mean, Evelyn. Please watch your language. Your daughter's in the car with us."

Amberlin chuckled. "Considering the news we just heard, I think my mother's language is both accurate and refreshing. Now, what do we do?"

"Why it's a pack of lies," Miriam said. "We've got to go to the police and tell them the truth."

"No!" shouted Evelyn. "No way I'm going to give them a chance to put me away again. I don't care if it's the Foster Flat jail or the Asylum," she said a little more calmly. "I'm free now, and I intend to stay that way. Besides, it wasn't all lies."

"What?" Miriam and Amberlin asked at the same time.

"I am armed and dangerous," Evelyn replied, "So keep driving."

It took two cups of hot tea and a half hour of sitting next to Tabatha's wood burning stove before she stopped shaking even though Tabatha had replaced the dingy blanket from the cellar with a freshly laundered quilt. She knew Tabatha was circling around her like a vulture around roadkill because she wanted to feast on the gossip of what had happened the night before.

Finally, she decided she was ready to discuss it, but she had her own plans on how the conversation would go. She knew her longtime neighbor was pretty much a loner. Oh, she attended church and did her community service like everyone else. But she never seemed to connect with people very well. Maybe it was because she was one of the few widows that lived in Golden Acres. Many of the other women felt threatened by her more youthful appearance.

Rose figured it was time to make a new friend, even if just for a short time.

"How long have we lived next to each other?" She asked as she took a sip from her tea. The warm liquid felt good going down her throat.

"Why, Rose, I'm not sure. I'd guess well over twenty years. Why?"

"Well, I'm going to need some help getting back on my feet, but I don't want to take advantage of your hospitality. Of course, we do have something in common now."

"Oh, what's that?"

"We're both widows."

Tabatha walked over and sat down across from her with her refreshed cup of tea. "Yes, that's true. I hadn't thought of that."

"Yes, but you know far more how to manage without a husband than I do. I've always admired you for that."

"You have?" Tabatha replied, an astonished, pleased look on her face. "Can't say many others around here have taken that attitude."

"Yes, I realize that. That's why I think it's important for us widows to stick together, don't you?"

Tabatha took a moment to take a sip from her cup before replying, "Yes, I'd like that. I must confess it's been a bit lonely living here all by myself. I've got plenty of room. You're more than welcome to stay with me until you get back on your feet like you said."

"Why, Tabatha, that's one of the nicest, most Christian acts anyone has ever offered me, and I am most thankful to accept." She took a moment to stir her tea. "There's just one thing I need to ask of you. I know it will sound, well, a bit strange, but I have my reasons."

"What's that, dear?"

"I need for everyone else to believe I died in the fire."

Miriam continued driving along the back roads, avoiding the major highways where she knew they were more likely to run into the authorities. After about fifteen minutes, Amberlin raised the question they'd all been asking themselves.

"What do we do now?"

"I'm not sure," Miriam replied. "If we go to the hospital, they'll arrest Evelyn for shooting Herb, and for taking us as hostages. Just give me a few more minutes to think. Luckily, Foster Flat isn't known for their crackerjack police department, so we still have time to come up with a plan."

As Miriam was considering their next move, Amberlin reached over and lightly touched her mother's uninjured shoulder. Evelyn turned her head towards her. "Yes, dear?"

"Oh, nothing," Amberlin replied. "I just wanted to touch you...to make sure you were real."

"Oh, I'm real all right," Evelyn replied, "but I know what you mean. It's a little hard for me to imagine my daughter sitting in the backseat and so grown up. For so long I've dreamed of holding you, but you've always been a baby. I guess I pretty much gave up hope of ever seeing you."

"Is that why you...?" Amberlin started but then didn't know how to finish the sentence.

"...Why I tried to commit suicide?" Evelyn finished for her.

"I guess so."

Evelyn paused before answering. "Yes, I guess that had a lot to do with it. I didn't think I'd ever see you, and if that was the case, I no longer had a reason to live."

"You'd lost your sense of purpose," Amberlin muttered as much to herself as anyone.

"What was that?" Evelyn asked.

"Oh, it's just something Papa Herb and I talk about sometimes...used to talk about." She corrected herself. She felt the ache in her chest returning. "He used to call it 'divine destiny.' He said we're all put here for a purpose, and when we lose it, well, we can feel hopeless and like life doesn't matter anymore."

"Well, that pretty much summed up how I felt." Evelyn reached up and patted her daughter's hand. "But not anymore." She gave the hand a squeeze. "I'm filled with hope now that you're here. I know that may sound funny considering I've been shot, wrongly accused of killing my father, and we're on the run from the law. I feel more hopeful and on purpose than I've felt for years. Go figure."

"Not funny at all," Amberlin replied. It felt so good to have her mother hold her hand. "I feel the same way."

Miriam glanced over to the two of them. "I'm sorry to interrupt your reunion, but I've come up with a plan."

"We're all going to fly to Acapulco where you have your second home," Evelyn joked.

"No, at least not yet," Miriam replied, smiling for the first time in several hours. "First order of business is to get your shoulder taken care of. I know where we can do that without alerting the law. I have an old friend; actually an old friend of my husband. They were in the service together. Canyon...that's his name, or at least what everyone calls him...was a medic in the Army. He's dressed more wounds than you can shake a stick. He also got himself in a little trouble with the law a few years ago, and there's no love loss there. He'll be only too happy to treat you without reporting it. It'll be his way of getting back at 'the man.'"

She glanced in the rearview mirror as she slowed down to pull to the side of the road, then whipping the car in a sharp U-turn. "Sit back and make yourselves comfortable. He's a couple hours away. I'll have to take mostly back roads to cut down on the chances of being picked up by the police. Also, be on the lookout for a pay phone too. I need to call my mother's next-door neighbor. She'll be able to let my mother know I'm okay. Together, they should be able to look after my son for awhile."

"That's fine," Evelyn replied. "When we stop for the phone call, it will give me the opportunity to get in the backseat. I'd like to visit with my daughter."

Miriam laughed. "Why sure. This is one place that encourages plenty of visitations."

A few minutes later, she pulled the Chevy into the parking lot of a diner with a couple pay phones out front. "I'm sure you have plenty to catch up on."

"You can say that again," Amberlin replied. "Like a whole lifetime."

Tabatha sat stunned by Rose's request, a swallow of tea stuck half way down. Finally, she shook herself out of her stupor. "Okay, yes, I guess we can do that." She thought about it a little longer. "But won't we need a body?"

"Good point," Rose replied. "I'm kinda still using this one." Then she remembered having the same dilemma several years ago when Missy and she had decided it was necessary to fake her daughter's death.

"On second thought, we don't need a body; we just need to convince everyone else that we have one."

"And how do we do that?" Tabatha asked as she leaned forward.

"Well, we can say you found my remains among the ashes and that it was such a horrible sight that you knew I wouldn't want anyone else to see me that way, so you..." Rose paused, needing a moment to think it through more clearly. "You had someone help you take it to the church."

"Sure, that makes sense," Tabatha said. "After all, I am on the committee that oversees such matters. No one would think I was doing any more than what I'd be expected to do."

"But you couldn't carry the body by yourself," Rose added. "That means we'll have to include someone else in our deception."

The two women thought about it for a minute as they sipped their tea. Finally, Tabatha snapped her fingers. "I know. Eddie Mulvich. He's perfect for it. You know, the Mulvich's older boy. The one that's a bit slow...well, really slow. He helps me around here all the time. Strong as an ox, but not much brighter. He loves me to death, probably because I'm one of the few people who doesn't treat him like a complete idiot. He won't say anything."

"Perfect," Rose replied slapping the table and startling Tabatha, who jumped in her chair. The two of them sat sipping their tea for another minute before Tabatha leaned forward again.

"Can I ask you a question?" Then continuing without waiting for a reply, "Why do you want folks to think you're dead?"

Rose took a last sip from her cup before answering. "There are forces out there...evil forces masquerading as good. If they knew I was still alive, they'd go to whatever lengths necessary to escort me to my grave. I just don't want them to have to bother with all that work."

As Canyon Green applied the last touches to Evelyn's bandage, Amberlin took a moment to study her mother's savior. Now, here's someone who fits his name, she thought. Of course, that figured since Canyon was a nickname, no doubt having come from the deep cleft in his chin. But he also had the greenest eyes she'd ever seen in her young life, and she was pretty sure he hadn't chosen his last name for that reason.

The combination of cleft chin and green eyes makes for a handsome man, she thought. Almost as handsome as Papa Herb. The thought brought with it a wave of sadness. It still didn't feel real that Papa Herb was no longer with her. Then again, what had been his last words? "Remember, I am always with you."

What had he meant by that? Had he not realized how badly he'd been injured? Or, as often was the case with Papa Herb, did he know something about life and death that she hadn't yet learned. She remembered one of her favorite stories in the Bible of how Jesus had risen from the dead three days after being crucified. But that was Jesus, the son of God, she thought.

But then again, hadn't Papa Herb often reminded her that Jesus, himself, said that we all had the same powers that he had exhibited? And what about that strange voice she'd heard a couple different times, including when it admonished her to turn on the radio at just the right time. What was that about?

The sound of birds fighting among themselves drew her attention to outdoors. She walked over to the window to see what all the commotion was about. Several small birds that looked like they were wearing black caps fluttered around a bird feeder. They looked familiar, but she couldn't recall where she'd seen them before or what they were called. Then she remembered.

They're Chickadees! As she had the thought, she felt a cold shiver run up and down her back. They're in the book! She'd completely forgotten about the animal cards and book — the only remaining things she owned that truly connected her to Papa Herb. Had that been what he'd meant? Was that how he would always be with her?

Amberlin rushed out of the room and ran outdoors to Miriam's car. She found her knapsack in the backseat where she'd left it. She pulled the book out and flipped through its pages until she came to the one with the picture of the Chickadee. Before reading, she took a moment to close her eyes, taking a couple of deep, cleansing breaths to help relax — just as Papa Herb had instructed her. When she felt settled, or at least as settled as she was likely to become, she opened her eyes and let them play lightly over the page. The first passage they fell on, stopped her in her tracks.

It read, "The appearance of the Chickadee is often accompanied by feelings of being cut off and out of touch."

Boy, you can say that again. She read on. "It is time to seek inner truth, to go within oneself for answers rather than to outside sources...go within your heart to find the truth and hold to it no matter what the outside circumstances."

She closed the book. Thank you Chickadee...and thank you Papa Herb. You are still with me, aren't you?

She closed her eyes and went within — another lesson her Papa Herb had taught her well.

Tap...tap, tap...tap, tap, tap. "Amberlin! Are you okay?"

Amberlin suddenly realized someone had been trying to get her attention for several seconds. She opened her eyes to find herself in the backseat of Miriam's car. She didn't know how much time had passed, but from how warm she felt, she suspected it had been quite some time.

She blinked several times to bring herself back from her quiet place and rolled down the window that Miriam had been tapping on.

"Sorry. I just needed some quiet time alone." She smiled weakly as she fingered the key that masqueraded as a cross around her neck — something she often did whenever she was troubled. It seemed to help her think somehow.

"Well, I can certainly understand, dear," Miriam replied.

Amberlin opened the car door and stepped out, placing the knapsack with the book and cards, over one shoulder. As the two of them started back towards Canyon's bungalow, Miriam placed an arm around her other shoulder.

"We've all had a very trying, traumatic day. Canyon has invited us to stay with him for a while. This place is pretty far off the beaten path and is as good a hideaway as any we could find."

"That's very kind of him," Amberlin replied as she leaned her head against Miriam for a moment. "Will my mom be all right?" Calling the young woman she'd shared the backseat with her mom felt strange but in a good way. She thought she would like having a real mom in her life.

"She'll be fine," Miriam answered. "Canyon gave her something for the pain so she'll be able to sleep. And that's what I think we should all do. Get a little rest."

"Then what?" Amberlin asked, still fingering the key.

"I'm not sure," Miriam replied. "What do you think we should do?"

As soon as she heard the question, Amberlin remembered what had come to her during her meditation. "Home — I want to go home."

"You mean back to Golden Acres?"

"Yes, that's right. My grandmother is still there. She may not know about Papa Herb yet. Someone should break the news to her."

Miriam nodded. "That's true, but I'm afraid it's also one of the first places the police will look for us. It could be very dangerous to go back there."

Amberlin realized what Miriam said was all too true, but then remembered the passage in the book: "go within your heart to find the truth and hold to it no matter what the outside circumstances." She looked down where her hand was continuing to massage the key and realized why.

"Papa Herb gave this to me awhile back." She showed Miriam the key. "He said that if anything ever happened to him to go to our special place in the woods where I'd find a box. This key will open it."

"What did he say was in the box?" Miriam asked.

"He didn't. He just said it was one more way he could help me fulfill my divine destiny.'"

Miriam looked confused.

"Oh, we were always talking about that. He used to enjoy telling me I had a special purpose to my life...even more special than most others. I don't know that I believe him, but if it's true, I'm hoping whatever is in the box will help me to know what that purpose is."

Miriam nodded. "Okay then. That's our plan. We'll rest up here for a day or two, let things calm down out there a bit, and then we'll find out what your grandfather left you."

She turned to leave, then stopped. Turning back to Amberlin she smiled. "It's a new day, Amberlin my dear. A new day for all of us. I believe your Papa Herb was right. You do have a special purpose for being alive. Let's discover it together. Now get some rest."

Three days later, Miriam's Chevrolet pulled into Sammie's, a locally owned gas station a little over a mile from the entrance to Golden Acres. Miriam turned around in her seat so she could better see Evelyn and Amberlin in the backseat.

"I'm going in here to see what I can learn. These small businesses are often a hub for the local gossip. Maybe I can find out what's been happening around here in the last few days. Evelyn, mind pumping some gas for us?"

"Sure," Evelyn replied, "if I can remember how. Just be careful."

"I will." She turned to Amberlin. "Do you need to go to the bathroom or anything?"

"No, I'm good," Amberlin replied. "I'll stay here out of sight, just in case there's anyone in there from Golden Acres."

"Good idea," Miriam said as she opened the car door. She strolled into Sammie's trying to look as natural as possible, even though she felt like she wore a sign on her chest. "Warning! Wanted Criminal."

She walked nonchalantly through the store's aisles filled mostly with junk food and other over-priced sundries that travelers might need but had forgotten to pack. With her eyes and ears on high alert, it didn't take long before she spied a copy of the local paper's headlines:

Fatal House Fire at Golden Acres

Her heart leaped into her throat. Could there be any connection? Certainly, this poor family couldn't be so unlucky. She walked over closer to read the smaller print. She skimmed the story quickly until her eyes fell on the name, Rose Gentry.

That must be Evelyn's mother and Amberlin's grandmother, Miriam thought. Oh, how am I going to break this to them? But even as she asked the question, she reached over and claimed the final copy. She grabbed a couple other items and headed to the checkout.

Placing the items on the counter, she reached into her pocketbook for some cash.

"And I'm also getting ten dollars of gas," she said to the old man behind the counter with Sammie embroidered on his shirt.

"That's too bad about the fire," she said trying to sound as nonchalant and unconcerned as possible.

"Yeah, I guess," Sammie replied. "You one of them?"

"Pardon?"

"You from that there community?" Sammie asked again pointing to the newspaper.

"Oh no. I'm just passing through," Miriam replied.

"They're a strange bunch over there...even for these parts. Still, a tragedy is a tragedy, I guess. That'll be $13.45."

Miriam handed him a twenty. Sammie looked at it as though it were counterfeit, and then with a quick glance at her, decided she was worth the risk. He placed the bill on top of the cash register drawer and gave her the change. Miriam pocketed the change and was about to leave when Sammie spoke again.

"Some say, it won't no accident."

"What was that?" Miriam asked, momentarily caught off guard.

"Oh nothing," Sammie hesitated. "Not that it matters, but I've heard tell that the fire was set by a crowd of irate neighbors. Not a very Christian thing to do if you ask me."

"I'll say," Miriam replied as she turned to the door. "Not very Christian like at all."

As Amberlin watched Miriam returning to the car, she felt a dull ache begin to build in her chest. Something's wrong. She could feel it even though there was no outward sign on Miriam's face. She tried to brace herself but didn't know how. How do you prepare yourself for the unknown? The best she could manage was to try to relax physically. She realized tension had already started to build in her shoulders, so she shrugged them a few times to loosen the tightness.

"What's up?" Her mother asked. "Is everything all right?"

"I don't know," she replied. "Just have a creepy feeling."

Miriam walked around to the driver's side of the car and opened the door. Amberlin noticed the newspaper and small paper bag in her hand. Why would she have bought a paper unless there was something about them in it? Was there a statewide manhunt for them, or something? She stared hard at Miriam, trying to find some clue as to the cause of the creepy feeling that continued to grow.

Miriam closed the door and turned to the two Gentrys. "I'm afraid I have some bad news."

"I knew it," Amberlin whispered.

Miriam stared at her before continuing. She opened the paper and showed it to the two women in the backseat. "I'm afraid there was a fire in Golden Acres. Your home was burned to the ground."

Evelyn and Amberlin both gasped in unison.

"According to the report, Rose Gentry died in the fire."

"Noooo!" Amberlin screamed. She shut her eyes, her body trying hard to protect her from the physical evidence of the photo showing the only home she'd ever known was now just a pile of burned rubble, but the image was already indelibly burned into her memory. There was no mistaking it. In the background of the picture could be seen the outline of the sanctuary that had somehow miraculously escaped the flames.

She felt the light touch of a hand on her knee. She slowly opened her eyes to find her mother's pained expression.

"I'm so sorry, sweetheart," Evelyn said as Amberlin fell into her arms sobbing. She was sorry not only for Rose but also for Papa Herb and for the life Amberlin had had with them in their beautiful home. It was now all gone...forever.

Time lost its meaning as the anguish and heartache consumed her. Even though she felt like the pain was more than she could stand, a small part of her also realized how good it felt to be hugged by her mother. The first time she'd been in her arms since birth, that time over twelve years ago that she'd often dreamed about. Finally, when the tears ran dry, and the pain had subsided slightly, she opened her eyes and glanced around to find a concerned Miriam holding out a handkerchief to her.

"There's nothing anyone can say in a moment like this that will help," Miriam said. "Just know that this too will pass...with time."

Amberlin nodded as she blew her nose and wiped the tears away. After another couple of minutes, she squared her shoulders like she'd seen her grandmother do whenever she had a difficult task at hand, and looked first to Evelyn and then Miriam.

"Okay...I know it'll be okay with time. I have to believe that even though, at the moment, it sure doesn't look or feel that way. I guess that's what faith is all about. So, in the meantime, it's more important than ever that we go to the Wild Woods, not just for the box that Papa Herb left for me, but...." She hesitated for a moment, trying to find the words. "I remember a few years ago when one of our neighbors died. Everyone was dressing to go to her funeral. Papa Herb told me, 'Funerals are really for the living more than for the departed. It's our opportunity to say goodbye.'"

She wiped her nose with the handkerchief before continuing. "I know it's too dangerous for us to show up at Rose's funeral, and who knows what's happened to Papa Herb..." the tears threatened to shut off her breathing again. "But I want to...I need to say goodbye to the only two parents I've ever known; at least known here in this waking world." She smiled to Evelyn, who nodded back. "So, let's go to the Wild Woods so we can say goodbye to Rose and Herb Gentry."

In an effort to avoid detection by any of the residents of Golden Acres, Amberlin directed Miriam to a side road. Papa Herb had once shown her the road that would take them close to their special place in the Wild Woods.

"We'll have to trek in from here," she told Miriam and her mother as Miriam turned off the car. "It's not too far, and there's a path that we can follow." She reached across the seat for her knapsack, figuring she might need it to carry Papa Herb's box in.

The three of them climbed out of the car, and Amberlin led the way. Luckily, they had a gorgeous spring morning perfect for walking in the woods. Amberlin could feel the magic of the woods helping to calm her as she started to put her life back in perspective. At the gas station, she'd received another assault of devastating news. It had felt like the evil wolf of her mind was about to devour her. But now, here in nature, her second home, she felt more at peace than she'd felt in days.

Miriam had made one other stop along the side of the road where a row of dogwood trees were in full bloom. She took a moment to cut off sprigs of the blossoms for each of them to carry.

"Dogwoods symbolize the crucifixion of Christ," she said as she pointed to the four petals of each flower with a small red tip at their ends. "But for me they also represent rebirth and renewal, and that's what this time can be for you and your mother." She turned and handed two sprigs to Amberlin—one for each of the deceased Gentrys. But when she tried to give two to Evelyn, she refused the second one.

"From what Amberlin tells me, Papa Herb never knew until the very last that I hadn't died in childbirth, and then he came for me. I will honor him for that, but Rose..." Her face grew red with anger. "I'll not honor her. For all I care, she can burn in hell for what she did to me."

Miriam nodded and dropped the sprig of dogwood blossoms on the ground.

Now, they strolled along the pathway lined with rhododendrons and mountain laurels until they came to a clearing in the woods where the large, moss-covered rock kept the rest of the forest at bay. Amberlin stood at the pinnacle of the rock where she had a clear view of the lake. Spring had been Papa Herb and her favorite time of the year to visit this spot because life seemed to be blossoming all around them. I guess it's also a befitting place to acknowledge the passing of a great man's life, she thought. She felt the tears well up inside her, but this time she didn't force them back but let them rise to the surface and overflow down her face. Crying is good, Papa Herb had often said. It cleans the soul as well as our tear ducts.

She stood there silently with her eyes closed, Miriam and Evelyn on either side of her. After a moment, she felt Evelyn's arm around her shoulder, and a moment later Miriam's arm around her waist. The three of them stood together in silent prayer for several minutes, each of them holding their dogwood sprigs.

How am I ever going to make it without you? Amberlin asked. You promised to stay with me, to help protect and prepare me for life and my destiny. She felt a wave of anger arise, forcing another wave of tears up and out. Then, after a moment, she felt and heard another voice so strong, she knew it wasn't just her thoughts.

I am always with you, it said. *I've only changed form.*

The message was so clear and in such a distinctive and familiar voice that it forced Amberlin's eyes open.

There in the distance over the waters of the lake stood Papa Herb. *I always thought this was one of Christ's neatest tricks;* Amberlin heard his voice inside her say, then a chuckle. *Spring is also a time for renewal of your faith and trust, my dear sweet child. Never doubt the power within you...to guide and direct you on your path. I will be here as well, but also remember to listen to your other friends.*

Other friends? Amberlin wondered who he meant? Miriam? Evelyn? Hannah?

Yes, those too, he replied, *but especially your nature guides.*

And with that the vision slowly evaporated into thin air, only to be replaced a moment later by a flock of geese flying in V-formation approaching the lake in perfect landing form. Upon seeing the birds, Amberlin knew immediately who Papa Herb was referring to — her nature guides, the animals.

"They have a message for me," Amberlin whispered, then glanced from side to side at her companions.

"What's that dear?" Evelyn asked.

Amberlin pointed to the geese as they came in for a landing on the lake, squawking over their success. She pulled the book from her knapsack. "A few weeks ago I decided to surprise Papa Herb on his birthday by memorizing what each of the animals stood for, but I've not finished yet. I just know that those geese are here to help me understand something important.

"What's that?" Evelyn asked

"I don't know, but this does," Amberlin replied holding up the book.

"I recognize that. That's my book of Animal Guides. Do you have the cards as well?"

Amberlin nodded as she took the deck of cards from her knapsack.

"Papa Herb gave them to me right here in this spot some time back. Of course, he didn't have any idea at that point that you were still alive." She held them both out to her mother.

"No, no, honey," Evelyn said, pushing the book and cards away. "He gave them to you, and so they're yours. If I need them for anything, I'll ask to borrow them."

Amberlin smiled, glad her mother was refusing to take them. "Well here, you look up the goose card while I look up what it says in the book."

Evelyn took the cards and shuffled through them while Amberlin paged through the book.

"Here it is," Evelyn said after a moment.

"Read what it says," Amberlin replied as she continued to leaf through the book.

"It says, 'Heed the call of the quest,'" Evelyn said, then looked up with a confused look on her face. "What quest?"

Amberlin shrugged but continued searching through the book until she found the right page. She scanned down the page for a moment allowing her feelings to guide her to the most salient points. Finally, she looked up. "Listen to this," and she read: "the call to the quest is being sounded and now is the time to heed the call." She read on: "That honking you hear is their invitation to follow them on the great spiritual quest. A journey has hints of fulfilled promises and dreams that only great quests can bring."

Amberlin closed the book. "We are being invited to experience new wonders and new possibilities. This is an opportunity for great adventure." At least that's what I'm getting from Goose." She looked first at her mother then to Miriam.

"Will you join me?"

As the three women stood on the rock saying their farewells to the older Gentrys, a dark shape looked on from the bushes nearby. Well hidden by the new spring growth but close enough to hear most of what was said, she smiled. A quest is it? So, that's what it is to be. Why, yes, I'd be honored to join in.

CHAPTER TWENTY-TWO
Epilogue

YOUR Divinely Inspired Purpose is more about who you are as a spiritual being and what you came to this earth to be and to experience. W. Bradford Swift

As Amberlin asked the question, they came together in a group hug, each of them moved by the sacredness of the moment. Finally, they pulled apart just a bit so they could see each other more clearly. Miriam spoke first.

"Well, I've come this far mostly on a wing and a prayer. While I have a young child at home that I also have to consider, the good Lord has provided for us up to now. I don't know how long I can stay with you, but there's no way I can just abandon you two at this point. I'm with you at least until you're settled somewhere safe."

Amberlin nodded, then gave Miriam a hug before turning to Evelyn.

"Well, I'm sure as hell not letting you out of my sight," Evelyn said with a chuckle. "It's taken us too long to finally get back together. I'm with you for the duration." The response won her a long, firm hug from her daughter as well.

Finally, Amberlin released her mother and looked around. "Okay, where do we go from here?"

"I guess it's back to the car and on with the adventure," Miriam replied.

"Yeah, I guess so," Evelyn agreed.

The three of them turned to retrace their steps, but suddenly Amberlin stopped in mid-stride. "Wait just a sec! I almost forgot the other reason we came here. Papa Herb's box." She reached around her neck and pulled out the key.

"Oh, for heaven sake, of course," Miriam replied. "Do you have any idea where he would have hidden it?"

Amberlin looked around at their surroundings, considering Miriam's question. After a few moments, she smiled. "Yeah, I think I do."

She walked over to the hollow log that Papa Herb often used as a natural bench. She walked around it a couple of times, then reached inside a hole in its side, praying that none of the forest creatures would be using it as their nesting spot. After feeling around for a moment, she pulled her hand out with a small wooden box in her grasp.

"Got it." She held it up so the others could see it.

"Humph," Evelyn replied. "I was hoping for something a little larger. Something large enough to hold Papa Herb's secret fortune."

Amberlin took the key from around her neck and inserted it into the keyhole. It fit perfectly, and within a couple seconds, the lock opened. She paused a moment before opening it, enough time to take a couple deep breaths.

"Come on, dear, open it up. I'm dying to see what's inside."

Amberlin nodded as she slowly opened the lid and peered inside.

"Well?" Evelyn asked. "What do you see?"

"Just a small book and another key," Amberlin replied, holding the two objects up. "No, wait, there's one other thing." She held up the other object as well. "A ring."

"Is that all?" Evelyn asked, visibly disappointed.

"Don't be so quick to pass judgment," Miriam said as she took the small book from Amberlin and opened it up. "This is a passbook for a savings account, and if these figures are accurate, there is over ten thousand dollars in it."

"Now you're talking," Evelyn's mood transformed immediately.

"And this key looks like it goes to a safe deposit box, probably at the same bank."

"But which bank?" Amberlin and Evelyn asked at the same time.

Miriam closed the book and read from its cover. "First Home Federal of Foster Flats." She handed the book back to Amberlin. "I guess that answers your question."

"What question is that?"

"Where do we go from here?" Miriam replied. "We're heading to First Home Federal to collect your inheritance, hopefully before anyone else finds out about it."

About the Author

FOR OVER TWO DECADES, W. Bradford Swift has been conducting an experiment: "Is it possible to create a new context for life that is true to my deepest values, my sense of what's possible, and true to my soul and spirit? If it is possible, what will be the results? Will it enhance my life? Will I experience a true sense of purpose and meaning? Will I know at the end of the experiment that my life has mattered?"

Becoming a writer of visionary fiction and non-fiction has been an integral part of this experiment, as was co-founding Life On Purpose Institute with his wife in 1996, being a life coach to assist others to create their own life on purpose, and training other Life On Purpose Coaches.

Since selling his veterinary practice in the late 80's to pursue a career as a writer and life coach, Dr. Swift has published over 350 magazine articles in dozens of national publications. Many of these have been part of a pet writing project: *Project Purpose: to write and publish articles about people whose lives are dedicated to a bold and inspiring purpose or vision.*

He is also the author of visionary nonfiction including: *Life On Purpose: Six Passages to an Inspired Life, Spiral of Fulfillment: Living an Inspired Life of Service, Simplicity and Spiritual Serenity*, and *From Spark to Flame: Fanning Your Passion & Ideas into Money-making Magazine Articles that Make a Difference.*

Dr. Swift attended Clarion West in Seattle to further hone his skill and passion for writing fantasy and science fiction. These two genres are forms of visionary fiction. Fiction that first and foremost entertains while also enlightening and encouraging the reader to embrace greater possibilities in their own lives.

Giving back to future generations of young adults and adults through visionary fiction and non-fiction is an integral part Dr. Swift's legacy of a life on purpose. To learn more about additional books by the author go to:

[Author.to/wbswift](http://author.to/wbswift)[1]

---

1. http://author.to/wbswift

Did you love *Amberlin: Divine Destiny*? Then you should read *Babble* by
Orrin Jason Bradford!

One young boy is the key to the universe.In this supernatural thriller, a young
boy is discovered to be the link between the human race and the farthest
reaches of the universe. For Bobbie Cagle, the normal difficulties of growing
up are overshadowed by his unique condition, being misdiagnosed as autis-
tic. Caught between his loving mother and those who would use him for
their own purposes, Bobbie stands at the center of the universe and forces
the human race to the edge of their own evolutionary line.The Lord said, "If
as one people speaking the same language they have begun to do this, then
nothing they plan to do will be impossible for them. -Genesis 11:6Upon the
Towers of Babel, the people of the Earth scattered, and silence fell. Now, on
the brink of a new age, the human race leaps forward into the evolutionary
void and changes the course of human history forever. For young Bobbie Cagle, the normal difficulties of growing up are overshadowed by his unique
condition. Placed on the spectrum, Bobbie's inability to communicate nor-
mally is misdiagnosed for years as Autism and masks the great part in human
history that he is destined to play. Unknowingly able to receive transmis-

sions from the farthest reaches of the universe, young Bobbie's life is forever changed when his unique ability is discovered. Coveted by those who would use him for their own purpose, Bobbie and his mother flee their home out of desperation and fear. In the course of their escape, the truth behind Bobbie's gift and the effects it may have on the planet begin to the reveal themselves, all the while the future of the human race hangs in the balance. Find out what fate has in store for the human race and grab your copy of Babble today!

Read more at www.wbradfordswift.com.

Also by W. Bradford Swift

A Life On Purpose Special Report
Clarity of Purpose: Don't Live Life without It

Amberlin Series
Amberlin: Divine Destiny

Standalone
La tua vita con uno Scopo: Sei tappe verso un'esistenza illuminata

About the Publisher

Porpoise Publishing is the imprint of indie author W. Bradford Swift who also writes under the pen name of Orrin Jason Bradford. It is best known for publishing visionary fiction--stories that entertain while also inspiring readers to imagine greater possibilities for their lives.

www.ingramcontent.com/pod-product-compliance
Lightning Source LLC
Chambersburg PA
CBHW032000170626
46807CB00006B/2580